Forbidden
Reward

Sharon Debisaran

Sincere thanks to my husband, children and my friend, Agatha, for their support.

Chapter 1

Kara Brinner was finally a first year student at Straveng University in Brevika, the capital of Mindalea. She spent her first day at school going from one class to another, thoroughly enjoying every minute of being at a top-rated university.

Years of preparation ensured that she not only qualified for Straveng, but that she was awarded a full scholarship. Since this was a rare enough occurrence, it was unlikely that she was going to let anything or anyone, side track her from accomplishing her goal. Kara was bent on becoming a scientist and landing a prominent position with one of the top, progressive, technology companies in Mindalea.

Even as a child she had a particular interest in physics so it was ironic that when she walked purposefully into her first class on the subject, her resolve to focus was completely shaken. All it took was one glance at a gorgeous, male student sitting at the back of the class to send a jolt of adrenaline rushing through her body. The fact that the man's eyes found and held hers in a brief, but intense gaze, only managed to make the situation worse.

Heat rose instantly to her face. Even from

across the room she could feel the electricity between them spark and crackle. In fact, the feeling was so intense that she was compelled to plop down on the first seat she could find; as far away from him as possible. Promptly turning her back to him, Kara tried to compose herself, but her heart was beating wildly and her breathing felt shallow. There was even a slight tremor to her fingers.

By the time she finally got her breathing under control, she had missed the teacher's self introduction entirely. For much of the class she could hardly focus on a word the man was saying anyway, she was too preoccupied with feeling like the stranger's eyes were boring into her back.

Kara was intrigued by the tall, handsome man and amazed at her own reaction to him. Although she was quite accustomed to receiving attention from the opposite sex, this was the first time that she was so affected by someone.

From his bearing and looks, she thought he must be at least a couple of years ahead of her at Straveng - maybe this was even his final year. Why else would he be in an introductory class at this stage in his education; unless it was to make up the credits he would need to graduate.

When the teacher's time was up and the students began to mill about greeting each other, Kara was immediately surrounded. She scanned the faces around her, disappointed that the man who had introduced himself to the class as Logan Ursin, was nowhere to be seen.

Logan also felt the jolt of initial attraction as strongly as Kara had. He thought that she was the most beautiful woman he had ever seen, and he spent long minutes trying to imagine her naked. When reason finally prevailed about half way through the class, he forced himself to face the reality of his situation. He was daydreaming about someone he could not have; a fact he should never forget. It was not permissible for him to have a romantic attachment to a Mindalean - especially now.

Logan was born and bred in Mindalea, but like so many other Giddians, he had managed to keep himself somewhat apart, even while living in the midst of them.

His mother was pregnant with him when she and his father first crossed the Alarius Sea as refugees from Giddia. Supposedly they were fleeing a socialistic regime, but in reality they were being planted by that same authority.

Each Giddian refugee had been coming to the shores of Mindalea for years with one objective in mind – to prepare for an invasion. Seventy years had passed since they were last at war with the Mindaleans, but the Giddians never forgot the injustice they felt they had suffered at their enemy's hands.

Having lost the war, they were driven far across the Alarius Sea to the mostly barren island of Rhinaris, while the people of Mindalea spread themselves over the vast expanse of the remaining land.

Once he was old enough to understand the differences between the two cultures, his parents started him on a course of training that would eventually allow him to take his rightful place in Giddia's hierarchy.

At a young age, Logan became part of the scientific branch of Giddia's military. He was placed in charge of the Dunlop Project which was now in its final stages of completion at the university. It would prove to be the culmination of the work his parents had begun years ago, and once the device was operational, the invasion would begin.

Logan wasted no time leaving at the end of the class. His position at the back of the room ensured that he had a full view of all the other students and it was soon apparent to him that he was not the only one there who was attracted to the girl. The last thing he wanted to do was to stand by and watch while others had the opportunity to meet the siren who called herself, Kara. However, before he could get out the door, he was forced to witness a number of male students converging on her en masse. The scene turned his already dark mood completely black.

Chapter 2

After seeing him in the class, Kara thought about Logan often and wondered if he was involved with someone. As the days passed she began to notice him everywhere on campus but she was not able to discern a significant other. Of course that did not mean that none existed because he or she could be anywhere Kara knew; not necessarily at Straveng.

Logan continued to seem oblivious to her despite the many opportunities she gave him to approach her. It led Kara to believe that he had no interest in her and the realization was crushing.

When she saw him again in the Physics class the intensity of being so close to him still had not let up. By the weekend, she was spending too much of her time wondering what it would feel like to be kissed by him, and wishing that she could run her fingers through his hair.

One day while studying at the library, she felt a compelling need to look up from the book she was reading. Logan had just walked out of the elevator and stood looking at a flyer on the nearby bulletin board. The mere sight of him set her heart racing and she could not help but be fully aware of her sudden difficulty breathing.

After another minute he turned in her direction and started walking directly towards her. She quickly buried her head in her book again while the colour rose steadily to her face. Was this it? Was he finally going to talk to her? She was after all the only one sitting there!

She did not take her eyes off the book, imagining him closing the distance with his smooth, long, panther like strides. As he got closer, the anticipation began to build even more within her.

When he was almost upon her, the feeling was almost too much to bear. Not being able to help herself, she raised her eyes to meet his. Even though he had been looking at her, he quickly glanced away before she could make eye contact. As he sauntered nonchalantly past her, Kara's face coloured even more, so completely embarrassed was she of her silly high school behavior and expectations.

Logan unlocked one of the doors that led to the private study cubicles behind her and disappeared inside, closing the door firmly behind him. After she composed herself sufficiently, Kara packed up her things and left quickly.

Although feeling very disappointed about the incident, her longing for him that night was even more intense than she had felt before. Eventually surrendering to her need, she dry humped to visions of Logan Ursin impaling her. While she found release, she was left with feelings of rejection and loneliness.

To avoid running into him unexpectedly at the library again, Kara began to study on the seventh floor. One evening, as she was returning to her dorm, the elevator stopped on the fifth floor and the door slid open. Logan walked in and for a moment they stood facing each other, alone in the elevator. After a cursory greeting, he promptly turned his back to her and waited in silence for the elevator to descend to the ground floor of the building. When the doors finally opened, he stepped out and walked unhurriedly towards the exit.

In that moment Kara understood that she truly did not exist for this man and felt compelled to face the reality of her situation. Although she left the library

6

dragging her feet dejectedly by the time she arrived at her dorm room, she was completely resolved to put Logan out of her mind.

As the days went by, she began a campaign to studiously avoid him. A few weeks later, her efforts were no longer even necessary. He had stopped coming to the physics class all together and she no longer saw him on campus which meant that Kara was finally free of Logan Ursin.

Chapter 3

A few days later, Kara was sitting in that same physics class when the first explosion rocked the building. Before anyone could panic, their professor pulled out a fully automatic, laser rifle from behind his desk and trained it on the class. "Everybody please remain calm. I need you to stay in your seats before someone gets hurt." His voice was so controlled that it added to the surreal.

At first the students were shocked into silence as each tried to grasp what was happening. There was the sound of guns being fired within the building and people were crying out in panic.

As the commotion surged up the corridor towards their classroom, one girl close to the exit cried out hysterically and bolted for the door. She was cut down immediately by a single blast from the professor's rifle. She crumpled to the ground and started to scream, while her lower legs looked as if they had disintegrated, leaving only charred, smoldering stumps at the knees. Kara was petrified. Her mind went completely blank as she, along with the other students in the class, stared at the girl.

Suddenly the doors to the classroom were thrown open, and Logan walked in. He was dressed smartly in a navy blue military uniform that Kara had never seen before, and he carried a formidable laser weapon.

The sight of him took Kara's breath away. She knew instantly that she had fooled herself into believing that this man could no longer command a reaction from her. She stared at him in bewilderment as he scanned the room quickly. Today she had chosen a seat at the back of the class. As their eyes met and stayed locked together (his filled with a sort of triumph, and hers with shock and disbelief), he moved towards her, seemingly in slow motion.

Kara was vaguely aware of more men dressed in blue entering the room. They bellowed commands to get the students moving into the corridor, but her entire being was focused on Logan. He made his way across the room, heading straight for her. Taking hold of her arm firmly, he exerted force to get her to move. "Come with me," he commanded.

His warm, firm grasp on her arm sent a physical shock through her body. She willed herself to place one foot in front of the other to follow his lead. Already most of the students were standing in the hallway where they were joined by scores of others who were pouring out of similar classrooms. People looked dazed while the girl who had been shot was being dragged along the corridor ahead by two uniformed men. She was screaming but they pressed on relentlessly with her.

Kara heard the frantic questions of people all around her. "What's happening?" "Who are you people?" "What do you want with us?" But their questions were only greeted with deadpan faces and silence.

Even though she had been quiet all along, she was finally coming out of her stupor. Logan, who had maintained his grip on her arm, was propelling her along with the crowd. Kara wrenched it from his grasp and hissed: "Unhand me!" She stopped and was looking defiantly at him, but she was infuriated to see a slightly amused smile play across his sensual lips. Raising an eyebrow at her sudden vehemence, he took his hand off her in an exaggerated gesture of resignation but in another moment he uttered a single command that brooked no disobedience: "Move!"

Kara felt more like staying rooted to the spot than obeying him, but she was pushed along against her will by a swarm of students coming down the corridor. As she was hustled out the front door of Grant's Hall, she noticed that Logan had not kept pace with her or even followed her. She was relieved and felt grateful for her anonymity in the crush of students.

People were still filing out of the buildings on campus to join the throngs as they were pushed along. Their eventual destination appeared to be the large, outdoor sports field near the auditorium which was beginning to fill up fast with bewildered students and faculty alike.

Occasionally, air mobiles would fly overhead, but they were unlike any Kara had ever seen. In the distance there were loud explosions as if bombs were being dropped, while closer at hand there was also the sound of guns going off.

For the most part people moved along quietly, despite the apparent confusion on their faces. Kara began noticing other students and faculty she recognized, dressed in the navy blue military uniforms. Other people who also recognized the faces tried to approach them for some answers, but the crowd was further shocked to see some of these unfortunate souls beaten and dragged away by the same people they trusted. Those who managed to pick themselves up off the ground were quickly marched along with everyone else.

A feeling of overwhelming fear spread like wildfire and quickly took root. Like Kara, most of the people were so bewildered that they moved along like sheep to the slaughter as they waited for their own military to step in and rescue them.

About fifteen minutes later, the field was almost filled with people surrounded by sentinels placed at regular intervals.

The captives had been separated by gender and directed to different sides of the field. Kara made her way towards the middle of the group of women, preferring to be on her own rather than to seek out a familiar face among the crowd to gravitate to. She found a spot on the field to sit, and wasted no time drawing up her knees to her chest and hugging them tightly. The temperature was cool enough to warrant a light jacket but most people had been forced from the buildings before they could grab extra layers. Like her, many now stood or sat, huddled over for warmth.

If any of the women fainted, they were left where they fell unless some of the others around them took it upon themselves to rouse and comfort them. No talking of any kind was permitted so many just stood around or sat and cried softly. Some clung together for support while others tried to distance themselves as much as they could from the rest of the group. It was not unusual for the smell of urine or feces to waft through the air, because some of the women were so scared, they had soiled themselves.

The crowd was already there for a number of hours without food or water before a stage was hastily erected at one end of the field. Soldiers moved about quickly, setting up wireless speakers as people stood up to look at the stage expectantly. Many were still in denial and were hoping that they would soon be told that this was all some sick joke.

Chapter 4

It was another half an hour before uniformed men began filing out of the nearby auditorium and climbing the steps to the small stage. Kara counted eleven in all. It was clear from their uniforms that the men were all officers holding various ranks.

To her surprise, she clearly noted Logan among them even from where she stood so far away. It was impossible to miss him standing erect and looking more distinguished than any of the other officers.

A tall, slim man with a narrow face immediately stepped up to the podium while the other men dropped back a pace, forming a line behind him. They stood at ease looking smartly dressed and imposing with their heads held high.

The tall man began to speak with a heavy Giddian accent. "I am General Atto Degan of Giddia," he said, with authority. "Giddia has invaded and already conquered large parts of Mindalea. Your military has been immobilized and rendered useless, and it is only a matter of time before all of Mindalea is under our control." He paused as he surveyed the stunned faces before him. Everyone including Kara felt that this just could not be true.

The man continued. "As you are now our prisoners, you will be treated as the property of Giddia." A murmur of protest went up among the people corralled on the playing field but no one dared to protest this announcement openly. "Those who are willing to comply, may find that their service to our great nation is bearable, and may even be enjoyable." He paused again and with a sneer, he focused his attention on the female captives. Many of the guards

12

who stood on the field with their guns trained on the prisoners, guffawed. General Degan continued in a cold voice. "Those who resist will be dealt with promptly, as many of you have already witnessed. It is in your best interest to comply and give up all hope of rescue. I can assure you that none will be forthcoming. Follow our instructions and no harm will come to you. Defy us, and you will suffer the consequences."

Kara took it all in but it truly felt as if she was having a nightmare. The thought that Mindalea could be invaded was preposterous. Yet here she stood along with so many of her fellow Mindaleans, surrounded by hostile Giddians. Where were their military forces? Could the general be telling the truth when he said that no one could be expected to come to their rescue? Giddia was considered so insignificant to the titan Mindalea, how was any of this possible?

Kara stole a glance at Logan as he stood immobile on the stage but he kept his head and eyes front and center. She was called back to the reality of the general speaking again. He had switched to a different language which she could not understand and which she could only assume was Giddian. It appeared as if he had issued a command because immediately, the male population of Straveng was led off the field, leaving behind about four hundred women.

There were only male soldiers and offices as far as Kara could tell and she could not help but notice a subtle change in the ones that remained to guard the women. There was a heightened sense of excitement and anticipation as they began to openly peruse the faces and bodies of some of the women.

The man at the podium turned his attention back to the women. They were unconsciously huddled even tighter on the field. "You are to stay where you are," he commanded. "If you try to resist your fate or run you could be killed on the spot."

The women looked frightened as their eyes darted from one uniformed soldier to the next. There was one standing just a few paces behind Kara who boldly made eye contact with her when she turned to look at him. As fear jolted through her, she quickly turned back and dropped her eyes to the ground. She felt her heart pounding as she resisted the urge to scream.

The tall man finally stepped down from the stage and was immediately surrounded by a sea of blue. A number of uniformed men had quickly come up and surrounded him. General Degan walked into the throng of females looking boldly at faces and bodies as he advanced. The women were in shock. A few minutes later when he emerged, his men were dragging away two, very pretty women who were struggling and screaming.

Panic immediately took hold of the group as the women surged like a tide against the men surrounding them. A number of them were immediately immobilized either physically by the soldiers, or shot so that they dropped to the ground screaming and writhing in pain. That froze the rest of them in place.

Besides being even more afraid, Kara was unaffected by the commotion because it did not penetrate to the centre of the crowd. Turning her gaze to the stage again, she saw a short, fat man step forward. As he walked by Logan he stopped and said something to him and then laughed but Logan only smiled in reply. The man then made his way down the steps of the stage and straight into the sea of women.

A few minutes later, he reemerged with a busty, tall girl that Kara recognized from her own dormitory. She was slung over the shoulder of another soldier who was following the squat man as he made his way off the field with quick, stunted strides. The woman did not struggle but Kara could see that she looked terrified, and that she was crying.

Her eyes fell on one of the soldiers who stood on the perimeter of the circle. He was looking directly at her with such a lascivious expression on his big, meaty face, that she felt the bile rising inside her. She was sure that she would never survive an attack from a man like that.

Acting as coolly as she could, she moved her gaze slowly back to the stage in time to see Logan, lithely stepping down and making his way unerringly into the crowd.

Even though he was heading in her general direction without glancing to the left or right, Kara did not feel that she had anything to fear. She was lost in a field of faces that was hundreds strong, many of whom were beautiful and sexy. But before long, Logan's determined strides were making a bee line for her.

Kara found this hard to believe. Was he really coming towards her or was there someone else that stood close by whom he had set his sights on? As yet he was still too far away for her to determine where he was looking and suddenly she was sure that she didn't even want to know.

She dropped her eyes to the ground and refused to look up again even when the women immediately in front of her parted obligingly to let him through. Kara was determined to hold her ground despite the sudden urge to turn tail and run. She did not even lift her eyes when a pair of shinny, black boots suddenly appeared in her line of vision and went still in front of her.

He was so close that she could feel his breath on her. In an instant of weakness she completely lost her resolve to stand her ground. Without raising her eyes to look at him, she breathed a single word in fear, "No," and she backed away from him only to come up short against a hard, unyielding frame behind her.

Kara did not even need to turn around to know who stood there. She was sure that it was the first soldier who had held her eyes when she turned around and looked at him. She knew in that moment that Logan had never lost track of her in the crowd as she had assumed. All he needed to do to find her was to keep track of the man who now stood behind her.

Chapter 5

Logan had been waiting for this moment a long time so he wasn't planning to rush it. From day one he had been trying to convince himself that Kara was a Mindalean, and therefore he had no business being with her. Yet he found himself constantly observing, following, and eventually becoming obsessed with her.

It had been agonizing knowing that he could not simply walk up to her and start a conversation. He felt sure that she would have been receptive to his attentions because she seemed as affected by their attraction as he was. Instead, she was destined to become a casualty of war. The thought did not sit well with him but he had not been able to come up with a satisfactory solution to the problem.

Still, it was difficult to keep away from her, even though he knew it was dangerous to continue to seek her out. There were eyes and ears everywhere at Straveng, spying and reporting on any behavior that was outside of the norm. In fact, it was Alfred Grute, the officer he worked most closely with who had observed him watching Kara. "We do not fall in love with them Ursin," he said pointedly. "We possess them, and we fuck them." The comment was enough of a reality check for Logan to back off completely from the girl so that he did not draw further attention to her.

An opportunity to intervene on Kara's behalf finally presented itself about a month before during a remote, face time conference he was having with the general and Grute. General Degan was in a very good mood because his plans were proceeding ahead of schedule - largely due to the efforts of Logan and Alfred. "Since you have both done so well, it is your turn to ask something of me," he announced grandly during their conversation.

Although Logan had been caught off guard by the general's rare, magnanimous gesture, he wasted no time requesting a Mindalean woman of his own choosing as his personal reward when the time finally came.

The general was surprised. "I would have expected such a request, if I expected it at all, to come from Grute, not you Ursin. Did you have someone particular in mind?"

"No sir," Logan replied promptly, instinctively protecting Kara, "But it would be easy enough to choose someone," he said smoothly.

General Degan smiled nastily. "You are certainly right about that. Mindalean bitches seem to be especially made for fucking. In fact I doubt that I will be able to settle for just one. Grute on the other hand may not find any to his liking. There are lots of blonds but very few who appear to be over six feet." The general chuckled at his own quip, while the other two appeared to smile indulgently. "Still, there is merit to your idea," he continued on a more serious note. "Maybe it is a boon that I can grant to the other officers as well. There certainly will be enough pussy to go around."

Logan cringed inwardly at the general's words. He had never grown accustomed to the manner in which his leader spoke about women. What was even more unsettling was that the disregard for women did not stop at the general but seemed a dominant trait among a number of other Giddian men, including Alfred.

In the end it was decided that each officer would be given the opportunity to choose a prize of his own. "Don't worry Ursin; you will have your pick of the pack as soon as Grute and I manage to choose our own particular morsels of flesh. I just hope for your sake that you don't like your cunt attached to very long legs and a blond head of hair." The remark was meant to poke fun once again at Alfred but the other two just smiled sheepishly as their general laughed.

Logan was relieved that he now had the means to acquire Kara, and he was determined to keep track of her. Especially on the day of the invasion, he did not want to chance another officer snapping her up prematurely.

He had managed to get Kara out of her classroom himself before needing to attend to other matters. The task of looking out for her from there had fallen to his adjunct, Jason Sivirt. Earlier in the day when Jason reported that Kara had instinctively made her way into the middle of the crowd he was relieved. He knew that it was the safest place for her and thankfully it would not have to be for long. He was only third in line to choose someone.

"Now that we possess them," Alfred had said to him before exiting the stage, "we can fuck them." While Logan acknowledged the flippant comment with a painted on smile, he was alarmed that Grute even remembered what he had said months ago. Nevertheless, his words chilled Logan to the bone as the reality of it sank in.

When he walked off the stage and claimed Kara, by Giddian law she would become his property. The thought had both excited and repelled him but now that he stood before this beautiful woman, his only thought was to possess her.

How many times had he despaired of ever

having her, while images of her being ravaged by another, or many, haunted him. He felt completely justified to take her now, convincing himself that if he did not, too many others would, and he was unable to live with that.

As he continued to remain silent and unmoving, Kara eventually had no choice but to look up. Logan stood before her, power emanating from every part of him. He was looking at her calmly curious to see what she might do, but his eyes blazed like an inferno.

She was still too stunned to move a muscle as he reached over to take her by the arm. Her voice finally came back to her in a rush. "No!" The little word came out almost as a plea, dripping with fear as her brain sent the right message to her limbs and she made as if to take flight. Before she could get far, his right arm crept around her waist and he drew her back tightly against him. Her back and especially her bum, pressing up against him, made Logan feel as if she had always belonged right there.

The allure of her sweet, warm body on his was so powerful that he closed his eyes slowly to savor it. It appeared as if he was trying to preserve the moment when in reality he was fighting for control. What he really wanted to do was to rip her clothes off and take her right then and there in the most licentious way. But he wasn't sure that he could deal with the consequences of such an action - especially if the other men thought he was in the mood to share.

"Are you going to cooperate and come with me?" he whispered in his deep, rich voice. "Or do I need to take you away by force?" Being so close to her, he could not help himself; he nuzzled her small ear and inhaled deeply, allowing her scent to permeate his body.

All the hairs on her body stood on end at the intimate nature of his act. As he continued to gently rub his nose and lips just behind her ear and down her neck, Kara felt a flutter of butterflies inside her stomach. She gasped and immediately bit down on her lower lip as she cursed the fate that placed her in this situation.

How many times had she dreamed of being in the arms of this man? Yet now that she had been granted her wish, all she wanted to do was to get as far away from him as possible. "No!" she ground out through clenched teeth again as she closed her eyes and reached up behind her to grab at his hair. He caught her wrist and brought her arm down and around to the back of her before she could manage it. He slapped a restraint on it, then caught the other and forced it behind her as well. Almost effortlessly he secured them both firmly.

As he turned her around to finally face him, Kara's eyes flashed fire. She yelled out in anger and frustration. "You fucking traitor! Let me go!"

Logan wasted no time hoisting her over his shoulder while she kicked and screamed. "What do you think you're doing to me?" Seemingly oblivious to her feeble assault, he began making his way across the field with Jason in tow.

They had just made it to the edge when all hell broke loose. The other officers on the stage had all moved into the crowd at once, claiming women and dragging them out.

Suddenly there was the sound of a shrill whistle and the sentries that were guarding the women broke out into a loud cheer. They immediately converged on the remaining females in the middle of the field and began tearing at their clothing.

Kara had never seen anything so horrible. There were screams everywhere as mass hysteria broke out among the women. They were tripping over each other to get out of the way of the charging Giddians - but it was no use.

Women were being forced to the ground everywhere while men tried to remove their own clothing enough to rape them. Others ran screaming in all directions before they were tackled and brought down to the ground like animals. Some were even assailed by more than one man.

"No! No!" Was that her voice screaming in desperation? Was that the only word in her vocabulary? She struggled and kicked as she bounced along gently on Logan's shoulder. He was walking easily with her but he had her in an iron grip so that her efforts seemed meaningless.

Kara could only watch helplessly as one man tried to grab a woman who rushed by him. Even though he caught her, the woman was able to wrench her arm free. Before she could get out of his reach, the man grabbed a handful of her long hair and pulled so hard on the strands that the woman was yanked off her feet. She went crashing to the ground, flat on her back. As she lay there stunned and breathless, the man immediately straddled her. He slapped her so hard across the face that Kara heard it clearly across the field.

Kara was barely able to stifle a sob as she watched the man point his gun at the woman. "If you try that again I will shoot you!" he yelled, and Kara believed him. He ripped the woman's clothes off her as two more men arrived. Leering at the woman, they helped to hold down her limbs while the man quickly unbuckled his belt. The woman was screaming "Stop!"

at the top of her lungs, but darkness was beginning to crouch around the edges of Kara's vision and mercifully she lost consciousness.

Chapter 6

When Kara opened her eyes, she was staring up at a high, white ceiling. She was lying on a large comfortable bed which dominated a small cell-like room.

She must have fainted she thought having no recollection of how she got there or if she was even on campus anymore. As she got up from the bed she felt a wave of dizziness that forced her to sit back down again. She had not eaten or drunk anything in a long time.

The memories of what she had witnessed on the sports field came flooding back to her causing her to feel anxious. In the dimly lit room she perceived a door and made for it straight away. It was locked of course, so she started banging on it. "Let me out of here!" she cried. "What do you think you are doing? You can't keep me locked up like this. Logan!" She called out loudly to get his attention but he did not come. His name sounded foreign to her ear even though she had said it many times in her mind.

It seemed like ages since she had first seen him in the physics class and had fallen like a ton of bricks for him. Now she felt ashamed that she could have misjudged someone so completely. He was just an inbred, barbaric, thug, she thought. "You have no right to keep me here!"

She pleaded. She got angry and threatened, but still there was no response. Eventually, what little energy she had was waning quickly. She leaned against the door and slowly slid down into a sitting position on the cold, hard floor.

The memories of what occurred on the sport

field continued to bombard her. Behind her closed eyes it was always the faces of the men that were the most distinct and frightening to her and she was thankful that she had blacked out before she could witness any more of the horror. She doubled over on the ground as the fear of the unknown overwhelmed her.

Initially she was relieved that she had not been one of the women on the field but now she was terrified of what she could expect. Was she destined to be molested after all? If so, by how many? And even if she managed to survive such an ordeal, would her torture even stop at that? Maybe they were not planning to rape her after all but being locked away in the room did not seem to bode well for her either way.

She was not sure how long she lay on the floor before she became aware of her hunger and thirst. As she raised her head from where it rested tucked on her chest she noticed a cup and covered plate on a small table on one side of the room. Curiously she got up from the floor with some effort and walked shakily over to one of the two chairs at the table. There was water and a veggie sandwich that looked scrumptious.

Suddenly Kara felt famished. With a gargantuan effort she tried to take her mind off the food before her. Why should she eat or drink to prolong her suffering? She had no clear idea about what was going to happen to her but she felt that putting nourishment into her body was only likely to prolong a fate she could not accept on any level.

She sat stubbornly at the table refusing to eat or drink for close to an hour. Finally she convinced herself that it would take more time and effort than she could afford, to starve herself to death. Once she had worked this out in her head there was no prick of her conscience when she picked up the tall plastic cup. She drank almost every drop of water in it before she started eating the hearty sandwich. As she ate, she thought again about what had happened. She had so little information though that it was impossible to come up with any theory that made sense for her capture.

Just when she was losing hope that anyone would ever show up she heard the sounds of a key being inserted into the lock. In another moment, Logan was there standing large and intimidating in the doorway.

Kara sprung from the chair and stood to face him as he looked at her long and hard. He came into the room locking the door behind him and placing the key securely in the pocket of his navy blue jacket.

Based on the thoughts that had so recently filled her head, she actually felt relieved that he was the only one who had come through the door and that he had locked it securely behind him. But as he unbuttoned his jacket and removed it slowly without taking his eyes off her she felt that her relief was short lived. Resting the garment at the foot of the bed he advanced on her with his deliberate, panther like stride.

Even though she had remained silent regarding him like a mouse would a cat that was getting ready to pounce on it, she finally found her voice. "What is going on? Why have I been brought here?" she asked when he was almost upon her.

"You are here because I wanted you here," he said with conviction.

"Why?" she blurted out, then she quickly raised her hand as if to stop him from responding to the question. "But really it does not matter," she said hastily. "You just need to set me free."

"To go where?" he asked. "Did you not witness the mayhem on the field earlier today? Would you have preferred to be among those unfortunate women?"

"And yet why am I here?" she shot back at him. He moved forward again slowly making Kara back away just a few more steps. She was completely surprised to feel the cold, hard wall at her back. How did that happen? When Logan first entered the room, she had stood up from the table that she could now see was behind him. She must have been retreating from him unconsciously as he moved forward.

"You are here Kara because Mindalea has just been invaded, and you and all the other captives are now considered spoils of war."

"Spoils of war?" she cried contemptuously. "What century do you think we are living in? There is no such thing anymore especially where people are concerned."

Logan smiled a little sadly. "Tell that to the women who are still entertaining the hordes of men outside that door," he said, gesturing behind him.

Kara was shocked into silence as his words were driven home. No, she did not want to be one of those women out there. "Why have I been spared?" she asked in a whisper.

He was very close to her now and looked both magnificent and dangerous at the same time. "Because you are mine," he said simply, as he closed the distance between them. He towered over her but he bent his face so that it was very close to hers as she pressed herself against the wall. He braced himself with both hands on either side of her.

"What do you mean?" she asked, hardly able to breathe.

"I mean that I have claimed you for myself," he said, looking at her intently.

"I don't understand," she said softly; bewildered. She was finding it difficult to focus on anything other than his sensual lips that were hovering so close to hers.

He reached down to hold her jaw firmly as he captured her lips in a full, possessive kiss. A shock of sensation traveled through her entire body. It was so overwhelming that she had to close her eyes against the intensity of the emotion. Her legs instantly turned to jelly and she could not believe that she was slipping to the floor.

Logan gathered her into his arms, pressing her firmly to his body as he deepened the kiss. Kara was too surprise to react. When his tongue darted into her mouth her eyes sprang open as she felt another shock run straight through her body to her groin.

There was the immediate sensation of need but unlike anything she had ever experienced. The man was overpowering and she felt completely helpless. He was supporting most of her weight as she was having trouble standing, but he did not seem to mind. The feel of his lips was extraordinary and she wanted to open her mouth even more so that he could have full access. Instead, she got her hands between them and was getting ready to shove against him with all her might. He captured her wrists and dragged her hands up and over her head where he pinned them against the wall with one hand.

She gasped at the unexpected move, and he used the opportunity to deepen the kiss even more. Her head was pressed firmly against the wall as he held her jaw again so that he could ravish her mouth more completely. The kiss was truly divine, making Kara feel lost, but he had suddenly become her enemy and she needed to get away from him not enjoy what he was making her feel.

She tried to bite down on his tongue but he broke the kiss. Holding her head firmly, he whispered huskily into her ears, his voice thick with need. "I would not do that if I were you." Still holding her pinned, he dropped his hand from her jaw to cup her breast. He sighed deeply as he closed his eyes and kissed her again.

Logan appeared intoxicated and Kara felt a raging fire in her groin. She moaned softly, trying to struggle free but she felt regret as well. What she would not have given before now to be right here in this man's arms - but not like this.

He whispered again in her ear. "Kara please don't resist me. I need you, and I will have you."

An agonized whimper escaped her, and she bit her lower lip to keep from crying. "Logan, please don't do this," she begged. "Set me free."

"I can't," he said, "even if I wanted to." He nuzzled the side of her neck and she felt that she could sense his own anguish. "There is nowhere for you to go, and I will not let another have you."

"But you do not have to do this," she argued trying to appeal to his reason.

He pulled his head away and looked at her. The fire that had burned in his dark eyes before was now all consuming. "I know but I have waited too long for this and I must have you now," he said in a strained voice.

He bent and scooped her up effortlessly before walking to the bed with her. She was completely scared and started to struggle. "Logan, please don't do this," she begged.

He stopped and looked at her again. "I have

wanted you from the moment I saw you, and I know that you want this too, so why deny it?" he asked.

"But not like this," she countered.

"Yet this is all we have," he said regretfully. "You can either be a willing participant in this, or I will bind you to the bed and take exactly what I have wanted from you all along." She froze in his arms. "Make your choice Kara. Do I need to restrain you?"

She looked deeply into his eyes and saw only determination there. It made her angry, but she sensed that there was nothing she could do to avoid what seemed inevitable. She shook her head. It was one thing to be taken against her will she thought; she definitely did not want to be restrained as well.

Logan's expression softened when he saw that she looked frightened. He laid her gently on the bed and began to kiss her in earnest.

"Kiss me back Kara. I know you want to," he whispered.

Kara shook her head in denial "No," she cried. "Not like this."

"It is all we have," he murmured again softly in her ear as if to convince her. He began to unbutton her shirt while Kara lay still on the bed, her eyes tightly shut. "Open your eyes Kara. Look at me," he commanded. She shook her head from side to side, her eyes still closed. He steadied her with his hands and kissed her again. "Respond to me, damn it!" he cried in exasperation.

Her eyes flew open and she saw that he was regarding her angrily. "Maybe I have not made myself clear," he said, with a hard edge to his voice. "You are my reward for a job well done and I intend to claim every part of you; with or without your cooperation."

"What would you have me do Logan?" she asked as her anger surfaced. "Spread my legs and allow you to just take advantage of me?"

He looked at her searchingly as if there was something he was struggling with in his mind. "Yes," he finally replied as if he had suddenly come to a decision. "If it means that you can find no enjoyment from being with me."

Her lower lip trembled, and she bit down on it to stop it from quivering but the gesture only inflamed Logan. He ripped the buttons of her blouse in his haste to expose her warm flesh to his eager hands. The sweet mounds of her breasts, trapped in a simple, white bra were enough to make him groan.

He had never lacked for female company and even had women who would think nothing of throwing themselves at him. Yet those beautiful, perfect breasts were making him want to drive himself into her without preamble. He could not think beyond the fact that he finally had his hands on her and that he wanted this instantly.

He watched her breasts rise and fall as she panted with fear. She was sultry to a fault and so completely fuckable that he found it difficult to think clearly. He bent and buried his head in her bosom, kissing and sucking gently on the exposed skin above the bra.

There was a sharp intake of her breath as she gave in to the sensation despite her fear. His cock was rock hard and straining against the fabric of his trousers. He had wanted to expose her body fully to his touch before he took her, but he felt as if he could not wait.

He got off her and yanked her skirt down her flared hips. Kara screamed at the sudden action. She tried to roll over on her side, away from him, but he quickly slipped himself free of his trousers and crawled back onto her. She was fighting him almost hysterically.

"Kara, stop this or you will hurt yourself," he commanded.

"I can't," she cried, her voice tight with fear. "You are going to rape me."

His whole body went still on hers as her words sunk into his conscience, threatening to get the better of him. He knew that she was afraid, but the sight of her almost naked body was still driving him crazy.

Logan forced himself to remember that she was supposed to be his plaything and a possession that could mean nothing more to him. "Yes I guess I am," he said resignedly. Slipping his hand beneath the mattress he pulled out a fabric restraint, making Kara's eyes grow wide with fear. Before she could utter a word, he straddled her, caught one of her hands and locked it securely in the restraint. He twisted the other end through one of the strong metal bars of the headboard and locked her other hand in place. She was crying and begging him to stop but when he produced a gag for her mouth she quieted down immediately.

She shook her head from side to side. "Please don't use that," she whispered.

"Well that is entirely up to you Kara," he said coolly. He reached down, grabbed her underwear and yanked it down her thighs. She whimpered softly as he pulled them off her.

"You are so beautiful," he murmured in awe, pausing a moment to look at her before he pushed her legs apart and slid between them. He was moving quickly but he wondered if she would say anything before he took her.

"Please Logan, I have not been with a man before," she blurted out in desperation. She was looking at him imploringly.

He stilled for a moment with an effort, and then sat up completely. Straddling her hips and supporting his weight on his knees, he removed his shirt before he slid up her body slowly and cupped her face gently. There was almost full contact between their bodies, except for her bra. "I know," he whispered. She went silent with shock. How could he possibly know? He smiled at her gently and brushed aside the lock of hair that had fallen across her face.

"I know more about you than you might think," he said, as he kissed her mouth again, slowly and tenderly. "I know this is not how you would have envisioned your first time, and I really would like to make love to you, not rape you," he said gently. "You can allow this and enjoy what I can do to your body, or fight me and suffer."

She looked deeply into his eyes and she saw the truth of his words. She knew that there was nothing she could do or say anymore that would prevent this from happening. She was lying beneath this man, almost as naked as he was, with his stiff, engorged member pressing against her abdomen.

"Just let go of the fear Kara, and let your mind embrace the curiosity and heat of this moment. I know that you have wanted me too. Well here I am, ready to take you to the stars if you would let me."

Kara said nothing but she continued to allow herself to be mesmerized. Her loins throbbed to have him inside of her, and he was asking her not to deny the feeling. He reached down and kissed her again. This time she responded a little. He nudged her legs gently

33

apart and rested between them, his mushroom headed glands pressed up gently against her wet opening. "Please release me," she tried half heartedly one last time.

He nuzzled her ear. "I can't," he whispered thickly, "I need to take you right now." His words flooded her body with heat again as he drove himself firmly and deeply inside her. He knew the moment he tore through her hymen and he absorbed her cry of pain with a kiss.

Kara felt him full and large inside her, stretching her painfully. She stopped struggling completely, and he too went very still inside her. As the pain subsided, she began to feel as if she needed him to do something desperately but she did not know what. When he started to move slowly, back and forth, with long strokes inside of her she knew that this was exactly what she needed.

"Open your eyes Kara and look at me," he commanded. She did. He was large and beautiful above her, straining on his muscled arms as he pressed down on either side of her.

As he continued to move, he did not break eye contact with her. Every time he trust himself into her, Kara felt a little closer to something deliciously indescribable, and soon she knew she had no choice. She needed him to finish what he had started. Unconsciously she bent her knees, spreading her legs further apart to accommodate him.

His rhythm increased, and she was thrusting her hips up to meet his driving motion. She wanted time to stop - for this moment to last forever, and yet he drove her higher. She yanked on the restraints, trying to break free so that she could wrap her arms around this gorgeous man and keep him right there between her legs. Her lust and pleasure felt absolutely wanton until all she could think about was finding release at the mercy of his hard cock driving wildly into her.

Then she was there, but the force and wonder of the sensation was too much for her. She closed her eyes tightly as she crashed over the edge of ecstasy with a cry of intense pleasure. There were three more firm, driving strokes and Logan was shooting his seed, deep inside her. He groaned softly with the sublime pleasure of release, and time really did seem to stand still for Kara.

When she finally felt as if she was coming down from the heavens, Kara knew beyond a doubt that she would spread her legs again and again for what this man could make her feel.

Chapter 7

Logan lowered himself gently back onto her body, kissing her briefly before he pulled on the restrains, deftly releasing her. He shifted onto the bed and pulled her smoothly into an embrace. He said nothing as he gently massaged her wrists. The restraint had sunk slightly into her skin as she strained against them while he took her.

Her cheeks rested against his chest and he felt her warm tears fall onto his skin. He held her even tighter as she continued to cry quietly from her sexual release as well as a host of other emotions including self-pity.

Eventually it was she who spoke. "How did you know I was a virgin?" she asked softly.

He chuckled low in his throat, and the sound was magical to her. "I am a senior officer of the Giddian military Kara. It is my duty to know a lot of things."

"I thought you had no interest in me."

Logan snorted softly, "I would have to be dead to not have an interest in you. And even then I wouldn't be so sure."

"Then why didn't you __" she stopped, too embarrassed to continue.

"Why didn't I take advantage of all those golden opportunities to approach you?" he asked, grinning mischievously at her. She blushed with embarrassment and he kissed her on her pert, little nose in a gesture of affection. "Because I couldn't. There are spies everywhere at Straveng and I could not risk having you come under undue scrutiny. But staying away from you was even harder to do. I obviously didn't manage it very well which is why you kept seeing me everywhere you went."

"You mean you were stalking me? she cried, in mock surprise.

"You could say that," he replied coolly.

Kara was not quite sure if she should be flattered or alarmed by this but it did not matter anymore. Right now she did not want to think beyond the fact that she was finally lying in this man's arms, and that he had just made sweet, magnificent love to her. In all fairness to him, restrained or not, what he had just made her feel, was far better than anything she could have come up with in her erotic fantasies.

They were quiet for a while. "I knew exactly when you gave up on me." She said nothing but Logan knew that she wanted him to continue. She was now resting comfortably on his chest as if they were long time lovers. "It was the night that we came together alone in the elevator at the library. I knew that you felt crushed when I did not show my interest in you, but the elevator there is the last place I would have wanted to approach you. It is constantly under surveillance. By the time I saw you the next day, there was a distinct change in you. You started to avoid me and I was terribly disappointed that I was no longer the object of your infatuation."

He was gently running his fingers through the soft strands of her hair as if deep in thought. "I was also a bit relieved too because I had no idea then how I was going to protect you once the invasion began. It seemed best that you forget me, but as you can clearly see, I never got over you."

She reached up of her own accord and kissed him full on the lips, making Logan go quite still. He was surprised by Kara's overture but he responded to her almost immediately, returning her kiss, eagerly; tenderly.

Their foreplay was heating up quickly when she disengaged from his kiss as if she could not help herself. "What will become of me?" she asked worriedly.

"You will be safe as long as you stay here with me." She was not willing to break the spell by spoiling the moment with further inquiry so she was quiet for a while.

She ran her fingers through the fine hairs on his chest. "How did you do it? I don't understand how all of this could have happened."

"Is it because the Mindalean regime is so almighty and invincible?" he asked sarcastically. Kara was surprised at the venom in his voice. It was true that her people paid little or no attention to what went on with Giddia, but she felt sure that they had bent over backwards to accommodate their refugees over the years. There were so many Giddians living among them that Mindalean politicians had begun to court their vote years ago, promoting many to prominence.

"That is not what I meant," she said defensively.

"Yes I know," he said with a sigh, as if he knew he was overreacting. "But you are still wondering how the mouse would dare to attack the lion right?" She remained quiet, unsure of what to say.

"Mindalea just grew fat and complacent resting on its laurels of a victory over Giddia," he said at length. "But we have been watchful. We won because we found a universal weakness in your people's technology that we could exploit. Working patiently and diligently, we were eventually able to take down the lion as it lay sleeping and defenseless." He spoke with unmistakable pride in his voice.

"What was the weakness?" she asked curiously

38

looking up at him.

He smiled at her. "Why don't we explore that topic some other time?" Bending his head, he kissed her gently again, relishing the soft, sweetness of her mouth. This time she responded, not wanting to be restrained again.

The feeling of him deep inside her still lingered, and she was surprised that he seemed to need her again so soon. She wanted to touch his skin, but she was not comfortable yet to indulge in this vice.

He needed more of her and as she opened her mouth willingly to his kiss, she heard him groan like a lost man. His hands traveled all over her body as he molded her to him. At the back of her mind, she wondered how this could feel so right when it was clearly wrong, but the thought was a passing one as she felt his need pressing up against her again.

Her loins ignited immediately. This time the anticipation of him eventually entering her was thrilling. He unhooked her bra and took it off completely. Her nipples were already taut. He bent to kiss and suck on them gently, causing a hiss of breath to escape her; the sensation was so exquisite. She reached for him despite her initial reluctance, running her fingers through his thick, dark hair, surprised at how soft it felt.

As she touched him, he groaned again and breathed out her name. It almost made her melt, making it the perfect time for him to slip his big cock into her wet pussy. It was as if she had spoken the thought out loud because that was exactly what he did.

They were lying together on their sides with one of her legs draped over him in an effort to accommodate him. As much as it felt good to have him inside of her again, she was unsure of how it was supposed to work with them in that position.

Rolling onto his back Logan flipped her on top of him. She cried out in surprise but automatically straddled him. The action broke their contact briefly, enough to make Kara feel bereft and cheated as he slipped from her body. All she knew was that she needed him back inside her.

"Ride me Kara," he said simply.

His words moved through her like a physical thing, heating and setting her body on fire. She did not hesitate. Positioning herself over his erect penis, she sank slowly down on to him, marveling at the physiology that allowed for such a large appendage to enter her slender body.

There was a soft sigh from Logan as he held on firmly to her hips. She felt her thighs; groin and butt, flush up against the warm skin of his lower abdomen, hips and thighs. The feel of him inside and against her was so intensely erotic that she suddenly had the raw, carnal need to fuck his brains out.

She panicked when she thought she would not know what she needed to do, but her brain and body were already instinctively taking her through a dance that was as old as time. She moved up and down his shaft, slowly coming almost all the way off, before she sunk down on him again. She gasped at the sensation of him filling her to the brim once more.

Over and over she repeated the motion as their rhythm picked up speed. She threw her head back, her eyes closed as she focused on the sensation she was creating for herself and him. Warm, large hands cupped her breasts, making her moan as Logan kneaded them gently. She leaned forward, bracing her own hands on his chest as she gyrated and ground herself down on him.

She looked at him and he returned her gaze, silently encouraging her eye contact. He is so gorgeous, she thought. She watched him struggle to hold his passion in check as he strained to give her pleasure.

Kara felt powerful as she continued to move her body up and down his rock hard shaft until she broke apart into a million pieces. She closed her eyes tightly to help absorb the intense emotion of her orgasm and was vaguely aware of Logan's hands tightening around her hips, sticking her on to him as he exploded inside her.

She collapsed onto him and lay there panting in wonder without bothering to release him. Stunned at her own audacity, she thought fleetingly that she was not sure why she had never done this before. As she felt him relax inside her she finally got off and tried to move away from him, but he held her firmly, sliding her down the side of his body to kiss and hold her tightly.

Logan was enthralled by Kara. Making love to her had surpassed his wildest imaginings, and he knew in that moment that he was not the conqueror but the conquered. His cock and balls felt wet with cum and he was sure that a river was also flowing down her inner thighs.

After a few minutes of rest he got up and scooped her off the bed. Opening the only other door in the room he walked into a small, minimalist bathroom. Moving with her still in his arms he entered the shower stall before lowering her to stand.

As he turned on the water, it was hot, and it felt good against their skin. He watched the water glisten on her red lips and could not believe that he felt himself stir yet again for her. He had thought to just shower and get some rest, but as his hands moved over her beautiful body with the soap, he could think of nothing but sheathing himself in her again.

He kissed her and she responded immediately, clinging to him. As the water cascaded down their bodies, he gently spun her around and rested his hands on her curving hips. He tilted her forward and she obliged him willingly, bracing herself against the wall with her outstretched hands. She felt his fingers slip inside her and she gasped softly, her blood igniting instantly at the invasion. She was already so wet and ready for him that he wasted no time positioning himself and driving his cock into her in one strong, fluid motion.

She cried out at his hard entry, the sound of her exclamation exciting him even more. Holding her firmly he took her quickly, enjoying the even tighter feel of her from behind.

He had intended to focus on his own pleasure because her body was enticing him to possess and fuck her hard. He was surprised to see that she too was building rapidly to a climax so that he only needed to hold off briefly before he was slamming into her, driving them both to boundless pleasure.

The friction of their bodies was so intense that they cried out in harmony. The feeling of her vagina still wrapped tightly around his cock was so amazing, that he continued to drive himself slowly in and out of her long after they had both come. Kara shuddered again and again as Logan prolonged their pleasure.

They were quiet as they finished up their showers, completely spent. When they finally returned to the bed, Logan was asleep within minutes.

Chapter 8

Kara waited by his side as still as possible for a full twenty minutes. She forced her body to relax and to regulate her breathing to assimilate sleep. Inside she felt tense and afraid as she tried to work through what she wanted to do. When she felt sure that Logan was asleep she slipped quietly from his embrace without waking him.

As she stood up and looked down at him in repose she was reminded of the proverbial gods of old; beautiful and sculpted. She was tempted to reach down and plant the lightest of kisses on his sumptuous mouth. As the memory of his lips on hers flashed through her mind, she felt weak at the knees all over again and regretted that she was not able to be with him under more bearable circumstances. But she was just his plaything, and what was to become of her once he had grown tired of her?

Soundlessly she moved about the room retrieving her bra in the dim light and putting it on quickly. She was relieved that her panties were still intact and she pulled those and her skirt on quickly. Her shirt was a wreck as none of the buttons remained, but she had already determined that she was going to be wearing Logan's jacket anyway. She picked it up from the foot of the bed and threw it on. She had not been brought into the room with shoes so she was forced to pad to the door barefooted.

She turned one last time to make sure that Logan was still asleep before she removed the key from the pocket of the jacket and inserted it into the key hole - so far so good.

When she turned the key, the lock clicked

inordinately loud. She closed her eyes and held her breath. Except for the loud beating of her heart and Logan's steady breathing though, all was quiet. She hazarded a glance over her shoulder again, relieved to see that Logan had not moved.

With trembling hands. she turned the door handle and breathed a sigh of relief when she pulled on it and the door moved without a sound. She opened it slowly; just enough to allow her to look outside and then to slip out quietly.

As the light of the corridor outside filled the crack made by the open door, Kara found herself looking straight into the sea green eyes of the man who had been with Logan earlier in the day. He was standing at ease and was regarding her with a slightly amused expression on his boyishly, handsome face as if to ask did she really think her escape would be that easy.

Kara was startled to see him standing there, but she played it off as nonchalantly as she could. Without acknowledging him, she closed back the door slowly and quietly. As she leaned against it, she could feel the hammering of her heart and her breath coming in shallow gasps at being caught. Her hopes were dashed on perceiving the guard outside the door but she still stood there racking her brain for something she could do to salvage the situation.

Could she try to attack him head-on? She would not stand a chance. The man was almost as big, and as muscled as Logan was. Could she try to entice and trick him into letting her go? She felt that the goddess of love herself might have a hard time of it from the determination she saw on the guard's face.

"Are you going to just stand there trying to figure out your next move, or come back to bed?"

44

Logan's voice cut through the quiet unexpectedly making Kara almost jump out of her skin. He still had not moved from the position she had left him in, but she counted herself a fool to believe that he was ever really asleep.

He rolled onto his side to observe her more clearly, propping his head on one hand. She could see even from across the room that the fire was beginning to burn in his eyes again. She had not moved, finding herself unable to do so again. He threw his long legs over the side of the bed and stood up. He was magnificent in the nude and already his member was rising to the occasion. He made a sound deep in his throat as if he had just eaten the most wonderful thing and was expressing his appreciation for the dish. "You look scrumptious in my jacket."

She doubted that. The jacket was clearly several sizes too large for her. It hung down the frame of her body as well as at the wrists. He walked over to her slowly and casually. "What did you expect Kara? That I would be fool enough to let you go? After what you have just done to me repeatedly, do you think it possible for me to give you up so easily?"

"What I have done to you?" she asked in a bewildered, almost breathless whisper.

She felt confused and a little affronted. Wasn't she the one who had been wronged in this situation? Wasn't she the one who'd had things done to her? But it was no use bringing that up now. By the time he was upon her his cock was large and erect and she felt a response to his need deep within her own body.

It was just as difficult as it had been before to have this man so close to her. The heat in her body started to rise and she continued to find it hard to

45

breathe. She hungered for him but felt ashamed of her intense desire for someone who had helped to bring her people to their knees.

He was smiling at her as he started to unbutton his jacket. "Didn't I just complete the task of undressing you already?" he asked, amused.

She did not reply. She could not. Her mind was a blank as she waited with full anticipation of what would happen next.

"No matter, I have no problems undressing you a thousand times," he said, in a seductive whisper close to her ear. Once again, his words ignited a flame deep within her. His fingers undid the buttons of the jacket expertly, brushing lightly against her skin as he worked his way down.

Kara could not help but close her eye because each time he touched her, she felt her body overloading with sensations. Finally, he slid the garment off her shoulders and allowed it to fall to the ground. He was so close to her that Kara could not help but notice that his eyelashes looked longer than most of the women she knew, but there was nothing feminine about them.

He had been focused on unhooking her bra when his eyes suddenly swept up to meet hers and he smiled mischievously. "See something you like Miss Brinner?" he asked smoothly.

Kara inhaled sharply to hear him use her family name and she was surprised at the little thrill that ran through her. When his thumbs brush the tips of her breasts, she felt a rush of heat that was becoming all too familiar. She closed her eyes again to hide the emotion that threatened to overwhelm her.

"Were you really going to leave me?" he asked quietly, as he continued to gently assault her nipples.

Her eyes flew open at his words. She met his smoldering gaze as he pushed the skirt and her panties over her hips so that they slipped down her legs and crumpled at her feet.

"Do you not see how much I need you?" he asked, gently pressing his hard member against her stomach. He kissed her with all the passion and need of a man who had been sex starved. He ravaged her mouth, pressing her into the door.

One of his hands found and cupped a breast, and he sunk his head to capture her taut nipple in his mouth. He sucked on it and tongued it until she could not help herself. She groaned and found relief from the erotic emotions that had been building inside of her from the moment he had gotten off the bed and made his way over to her.

He captured her mouth again in a hungry, urgent kiss, this time she returned it with ardor. He hesitated only for a moment, surprised at her reaction, before he nudged her legs apart. Kara thought with relief and excitement that he meant to fuck her right up against the door. She was ready for it and she welcomed the release his cock would finally bring to her fevered body.

Standing with her legs spread apart made her need for him feel even more intense. When he placed his hands just under her buttocks and lifted her up she could hardly wait for him to be inside her. Instead, he positioned her high up on his body, resting her moist pussy against his flat abdomen. He closed his eyes, savoring her heat.

"Wrap your legs around me," he commanded in a low, ragged voice.

The feel of her hot, moist aperture so close to

his penis was maddening for them both. She obeyed him instantly, automatically wrapping her arms around his neck as well. He enclosed and held her tightly to his body.

"I do so want to fuck you right up against this door," he murmured hotly in her ear. "But I want to do something else even more."

Kara could not fathom what he could possibly want to do more than fuck her right then and there. She was finding it impossible to focus on anything else herself. He turned and walked with her swiftly to the bed, draping her on it so that her legs hung over the side.

She lay there, fully exposed to him, and it was all Logan could do to not impale her instantly. Instead, he knelt between her legs quickly. Before she could clearly perceive what he was going to do, his mouth found her pussy.

She cried out in surprise as he boldly took in a mouthful of her hot, sweet sex. She was rising from the bed to try and push him away, but he broke his contact and slid up her body until his face was just inches away from hers.

"You are the sweetest thing I have ever tasted," he whispered. "Please don't deny me this pleasure."

Her lips were trembling with emotion. The act was more intimate than she could have imagined but his eyes were so sincere that she could refuse him nothing. She nodded her head almost imperceptibly. With a smile, he whispered: "Just enjoy," before he slipped back down her body.

What followed was the most tantalizing, agonizing experience Kara had ever had. After only a short while, she raised herself on an elbow so that she could put her other hand on the back of his head, as she gyrated under the assault of his expert mouth and tongue. She moaned with such intense longing that the sound startled her.

She started begging him: "Please. Please Logan." What was she begging him for? She was not quite sure. All she knew was that she needed him so desperately again that she thought she would die if she could not have him inside her. After what felt like an eternity of the most exquisite torture and fervent pleading on her part, he finally rose up and slipped his hard cock inside her more than ready passageway.

She cried out her relief at the feel of him filling her. She grabbed his arms as he braced his weight on the bed and drove himself steadily in and out of her. She came violently within just a few strokes, the intensity of the sensation causing her toes to curl. He stilled in her as she shuddered and cried out his name. "Oh Logan!" It was the sweetest sound he had ever heard. As she returned from the ether to rejoin him, he whispered in her ear. "I can't tell you how enjoyable that was."

She kissed him, her gratitude for what he had just done in every flick of her small tongue in his mouth. Now it was his turn to moan. Without breaking the contact, he nudged her gently to shimmy higher onto the bed so that he could get into it more comfortably. He was very aware of his hard cock still inside her as he grinned down at her for the first time. Kara felt as if the heavens had suddenly opened and an angel was gracing her with his mirth. "Shall we see if you are multi-orgasmic?" he asked.

She could not help but smile as he started a slow rhythmic dance inside her again, taking his time to enjoy the friction of moving in and out of her. This time his love making was agonizingly slow and Kara could not believe that she was climbing again so soon.

He watched her expressive face, enjoying the anticipation he saw building there as he increased his rhythm. She was beautiful and sexy beyond anything he knew. He never wanted to let her go. He felt her vaginal walls tighten and relax around his straining cock and he worked with almost inhuman determination to keep from exploding inside her prematurely. When he eventually saw that she was on the verge of coming, he felt both disappointment and relief. Relaxing his mental hold on his body they climaxed together.

"As much as you are likely to have a leisurely day tomorrow, some of us do have jobs to attend to," Logan said after they had both caught their breath and were resting on the pillows. "Can I trust you this time to lay with me here until the morning or would I need to bind you to this bed again?"

She looked at him sincerely. "I will stay."

"Thank you." he said, holding her to him as he prepared to fall asleep. Kara too, finally allowed herself to feel her exhaustion and have sleep claim her.

Chapter 9

All too soon she awoke to the sounds of running water. The door to the bathroom was closed and Logan was not next to her. Even though nothing had changed in the room to indicate whether it was day or night, Kara had to guess that it was the morning if Logan was up and showering.

As she lay on the bed she could feel a slight throbbing pain between her thighs. She thought about the time when one of her friends had told her about her own sexual experiences that led to becoming sore. Marcy was proud to relate the details of her encounter but Kara could only feel dismay at her own predicament.

She was assailed by memories of the last twenty-four hours, reliving the horror of the invasion and the episode she had witnessed on the sports field. She was desperately trying to avoid turning her thoughts to what had happened between her and Logan last night but when she could no longer manage it, she felt nothing but self-revulsion at being weak. Talk about sleeping with the enemy, she thought. She had epitomized the expression with her wanton nature; exercising no self-control. It was embarrassing.

Logan made an appearance just then toweling his dark, wavy hair, but Kara found that she could hardly face him. She had gotten up hastily and thrown on her underwear, skirt and torn top while he was still in the bathroom. Before he could address her, she dashed past him, relieved that there was actually a lock on the inside of the bathroom door. Turning it, she wasted no time before retching loudly into the commode. She felt sick to the pit of her stomach.

51

Logan knocked on the door. "Kara, are you alright?" There was natural concern in his voice, but she could not bear to have him come in; or to go out there to face him, for that matter.

"I'll be fine," she managed, before throwing up again into the toilet. Nothing much came out. She had eaten only a sandwich anyway since breakfast the previous day. "I just need a few moments to myself."

There was a short pause on the other side of the door. "I have to go. Will you be out soon?"

"No," she cried shakily. "I'm afraid not."

There was another pause that was longer this time. Kara held her breath and prayed. For what? She was not really sure.

"Ok then," he said reluctantly, with evident disappointment. "I will see you later today. Be sure to eat and rest."

Kara felt a wave of nausea again at his words. *Eat and rest* she thought in disgust, so that he could go at it all over again while having the satisfaction of knowing that her body would betray her once more.

She felt completely depressed. Was this to become her new life? To be kept a prisoner in a windowless room and take nourishment so that she would have the energy and stamina to withstand one night of fucking after another. And when Logan eventually grew tired of her, would she simply be discarded or would she be handed off to a platoon of men.

It was quiet outside as she made her toilet. Relieved to be finally left alone she stood in front of the mirror and looked at her reflection. She could hardly recognize the woman staring back at her. Flashes of Logan making love to her crowded into her mind. She cringed as her body tingled all over, immediately betraying her. She put her hands to her head and closed her eyes tightly as if she could block out the images raging through it.

The girl in the mirror was crying. How could she ever face Logan again knowing that she was powerless against his advances? She just wanted to die in that very moment.

Reaching up on impulse, she opened the mirrored door to the cabinet over the sink and froze. Inside were the regular items that a man might need in the bathroom, but interestingly, there was also a manual razor. It was the kind she had not seen since she was a child when her grandfather had insisted on using one over the latest electronic models. But what was a young man like Logan doing with one?

A quick look in the cabinet revealed that there were no electronic bathroom items of any kind. Her culture relied so much on electronics that it looked strange for none to be present in any part of their living space - especially the bathroom.

Kara's eyes were drawn back to the razor as if by a magnet. She removed the blade with trembling hands. Before she allowed herself to think about what she was doing, she ran the sharp edge of the exposed blade across her wrist. She was surprised to see the rich, red blood well up immediately and became alarmed when it began to flow freely; dripping to the floor.

What had she done? She had gone and killed herself. Logan was gone and there was no one to save her. She thought that she would be relieved by her action, but all she felt was panic and strangely regret that she would never see Logan again.

Suddenly she saw only darkness. She backed

away from the mirror and slammed into the closed door of the bathroom before collapsing to the floor; unconscious.

Chapter 10

Jason had been spelled by another sentry for a few hours just after Kara had presented herself at the door the night before. By early morning he was back at his post so that he could be on spot when Captain Ursin emerged from the room.

Logan came out looking relaxed but a little preoccupied as breakfast arrived for two. He motioned for the attendant to leave the cart and then turned his attention to Jason. "I think you would serve me better by staying here today. I will be fine on my own. She is in the bathroom. Stay with her though and keep an eye on her. Make sure she eats and rests. I have to go. I am late, but I will check in on her around lunch time." Jason nodded as Logan started down the corridor briskly. He turned around as if he suddenly remembered something. "Oh, and have someone replace the bed sheets."

Jason saluted again as Logan continued on his way. He had been tempted to ask how he had enjoyed his night with Kara when he first came out of the room. It was something he might have done before he became Logan's personal aid. Now, there was always the need to keep their relationship professional.

He wheeled the breakfast cart into the room and managed to close and lock the door just as he heard the toilet flush. Leaving the cart at the door, he stood at ease but felt a little embarrassed about being in the room alone with Kara. It was one thing to observe her from afar, and covertly, but another to share the same space with her openly.

As per Logan's instructions, he had gathered intelligence on her; following her unseen for at least a month; reporting to him on her every move. At first Jason had found her beautiful, but as time progressed he became infatuated with her. It was not unexpected, especially since she was so lovely, but he was always mindful that Kara did not belong to him.

He knew that his captain's interest in her went well beyond simple entertainment and possession. It was dangerous for Logan to attach such strong feelings to a Mindalean but Jason would never dream of questioning him.

"I would not trust this task of watching over her to anyone else," Logan said to him yesterday when they first brought Kara into the room and deposited her, unconscious on the bed. "No matter what is asked of you, can you see yourself serving me unconditionally in this matter?"

Jason had nodded without hesitation but now he was having mixed feelings about babysitting his captain's property. A part of him felt that he could be doing so many more important things to further his people's cause yet he could think of nowhere else he'd rather be.

As much as it was difficult for him to hold his own feelings for Kara in check, he was ready to do anything for his captain. If that meant guarding her and possibly even giving up his life for her, then that was what he was prepared to do.

Jason was curious about why Logan needed the bed sheets changed. They looked clean from where he was standing and the couple had only spent one night on them. On a whim, he walked over to the bed and gently scooped the flat sheet and cover away. His hand stopped in mid-air, his mouth open in surprise. There was a deep, red blot on the sheet below. She was a virgin? Incredible!

He wondered if the stain could have come from something Logan did to hurt her. He immediately squelched the thought knowing it was unlikely that his captain would mistreat Kara. The stain was also the right distance from the bed head for her height.

In the time that he had followed her, it was true that he had never seen her go out on a date or show a particular interest in anyone. Still, it was a shock to have actual proof of her celibacy. How was it possible that such a fine woman had remained unblemished for so long? Had Logan known all along that she was a virgin? Jason felt sure of it. The captain had been too nonchalant when he asked him to make sure that the cleaning staff changed the sheets.

Jason felt something protective stir deep within him for the girl, but he repressed it immediately. He threw back the sheet to cover up the spot and strode back to his sentinel position by the entrance to the room.

He heard her crying softly in the bathroom and it tugged at his heart. His need to go to her and try to console her was almost overpowering but he stood his ground knowing that it was not his place to do so. Besides, what could he possibly say to make this situation any better?

When she had first awoken yesterday from her faint he had stood right outside the door listening to her alternately pleading and demanding to be set free. She had banged on the door incessantly carrying on for so long that he could not help but admire her determination and spirit. It was too bad that she now seemed broken.

After all was said and done, it did not matter

how much Logan managed to protect and shield her; she was still a captive, and now she had been taken advantage of. While Jason could think of at least a dozen attractive women who would have welcomed Logan to their beds, none of them could hold a candle to Kara.

He started to get a little uneasy because he had not heard anything from the bathroom in the last couple of minutes. Suddenly there was a loud thud against the door that made it rattle. He knew immediately that something was very wrong.

He crossed the room quickly and banged loudly on the door. "Miss, are you okay?" he asked, urgently. There was no response.

Jason felt his heart begin to hammer. He tried the door handle but it was locked. "Kara, are you okay?" He called out more insistently, not even aware that he was using her given name, a thing he would only dare to do in his own head.

"Open the door Kara," he commanded, but there was still no response.

He grew anxious. Should he break down the door? What if she was hurt on the other side? Would he harm her even more by forcing the door? Swearing he drew his gun and leaning against the wall, he shot the lock off the door with a single blast. Opening it slowly he managed enough space to squeeze through before it was blocked on the other side. He was completely unprepared for the sight that greeted him.

Kara's slight body lay pale and unconscious on the ground. Her shirt had fallen completely open and there was a large smear of blood across her chest and the white bra she wore. His heart felt like it was in his throat as he stooped quickly to look for a wound on her chest. Then he saw the blood flowing from her wrist while the razor lay close by.

"Shit! Shit!" he cried. Pulling a large handkerchief from his jacket pocket, he tied her slender wrist quickly. For a moment he was completely unsure of what to do. He could call for help but it would be too late before anyone arrived.

Scooping her up from the floor like a feather, he almost ran out of the bathroom with her. The room door was locked making him swear again. He fumbled for the key in his pocket while still holding her. He was exasperated that his hand appeared less than steady and that he had to attempt getting the key into the lock a couple of times.

Logan worked in the same building but there was no time to alert him. Thankfully, the mediunit was just next door, yet even that seemed like a long shot to him. She had already lost a considerable amount of blood.

He was relieved that the elevator doors opened instantly when he pressed the button. Within a minute he was already outside the building, running with her in his arms.

When he got to the mediunit he made it a point to inform the attendants that Kara belonged to Captain Ursin. She was hustled into a situation room immediately, a crowd of medical staff swarming around her.

Once he had delivered her into their competent hands. Jason finally turned his attention to contacting Logan. As the signal was going through, he braced himself, dreading the reaction the captain would have to his news.

Chapter 11

Logan left Kara, feeling as if he was walking on top of the world. The time he had spent with her had turned out better than he had dared to hope. Despite being a captive and a virgin she had floored him with her passion.

His jubilant feelings and the images of their night together kept creeping into his mind making it difficult to focus on work. He felt a bit uneasy that she seemed unwell when he left but Logan knew if something was really wrong Jason would be communicating with him. As if on cue, his PI pinged. "Ursin here."

"Sir, it's Sivirt."

Logan wondered if Jason was already calling to request a change in assignment. When there was too long a pause for his liking, fear began to spread quickly through him.

"What is it Jason? Is she unwell?" he asked in a tight voice.

"Yes sir," Jason said hesitantly. "You could say that. I am at the mediunit. She slit her wrist with a razor."

"What!" Logan leaped from his chair making heads everywhere turn in curiosity. He was not sure what he expected but it certainly was not that.

"She was still alive when I brought her in sir," Jason hastened to reassure him. "They are working to try and save her now."

"Where are you exactly?" Logan asked urgently as he ran for the door. "I am coming to you directly."

Logan raced across the distance between the two buildings, wondering how he could be so stupid to leave the razor in the bathroom. He had meant to go back for it once he had showered and spoken to Kara but she had rushed passed him and locked herself in the bathroom. He had been late and had not spared another thought for it.

He was shocked that Kara had tried to take her life and was even more so by his own reaction to the news. Why did she have to do something like this? Had he completely misjudged her reaction to him last night? Had the experience been so unbearable for her?

He remembered her that morning racing by him, almost unable to meet his eyes; her dry heaving into the toilet and her refusal to say much when he asked if she was alright. Did she have a belated attack of conscience over giving in to him last night? Was she ashamed of how strong her own needs were? What principle of hers could have been so great that she chose suicide over being with him? Had he ill treated her in some way?

He remembered restraining her to the bed and he felt ashamed of the act but he did not think it qualified as actually hurting her. The scenario that was one of the harder ones to face was wondering if she had just faked her pleasure to put him off his guard so that she could do something like this.

By the time he joined Jason, Logan was almost out of breath from hurrying. Because of his thoughts on his trek across, he was an absolute wreck. It was enough to cause a look of deep concern to cross Jason's face fleetingly. Logan's agitation was showing too blatantly on his face and in his manner. "Where is she?" he demanded.

"They have taken her into situation room four. They will not allow you in there," Jason said, as Logan

61

immediately tried to get by him. He was keenly aware of the need for his captain to show self-restraint.

"But I must see her," Logan cried urgently.

"Captain," Jason said simply, but the tone of his voice was enough to make Logan stop and refocus his attention on his adjunct. Jason glanced around and then said to him in a low voice: "It will not do to show such concern over a woman that you were granted access to only yesterday."

Logan was thunderstruck. Jason was right. He was behaving as though Kara was his consort and not his property. He could not allow his comrades to see that he might have deeper feelings than was permitted for a Mindalean female. The professional veneer was back on his face in an instant. "What would you have me do?" he asked Jason in resignation.

They were both aware of the role reversal that had occurred. Now it was Logan who appeared willing to have Jason issue an order that he could follow. He did not trust himself to think logically in the moment.

"Go back to work and I will keep you posted on her progress," Jason said.

Logan stayed rooted to the spot as if unwilling to accept Jason's suggestion. He glanced at the situation room door which stood just a short distance away and worked on repressing the urge to bound across the hall and throw open the door.

Jason was able to read his body language easily enough so he tried again. "You are just a building away Logan. There is nothing you can do here right now." They stood face to face, about the same height and close enough in body type to be related. They were both very aware that Jason had used his first name to get his attention - something that he had not done in a long time.

"I will alert you as soon as there is some news to share."

Logan nodded reluctantly as he struggled inwardly for control. "What happened?" Knowing that he could not get the captain to leave without additional information, Jason quickly brought him up to speed in a hushed tone.

Logan was stunned that Kara had acted so quickly and decisively to take her life. He cursed himself again for being a fool to think that she had enjoyed their night together.

Chapter 12

After leaving the mediunit, Logan made his way to the room he had shared with Kara. The door was still ajar as was the one leading into the bathroom. Walking towards it, he saw where Jason had shot the lock off.

As he entered, he could not help but lean against the wall, shocked at the large pool of blood on the tiled floor. The razor lay idly by while the edges of the pool were smeared; possibly from when Jason had lifted Kara into his arms to carry her out of the room. Tears sprang to his eyes, surprising him, but he was beginning to feel utter desolation at the thought that he could lose her.

He stayed there for several minutes before he used his PI to call for a cleanup crew. Picking up the razor, he washed it clean at the sink, dried, and pocketed it.

As he passed by the untouched breakfast tray, he felt another pang of guilt. Kara had eaten only a sandwich since yesterday so she could be weak. His heart sank even further as he thought of her in the situation room with the medical staff struggling to save her life, but by the time he returned to his desk, Logan was fully composed.

As the day wore on, he received messages on his PI regularly from Jason. Almost three hours later he finally heard that Kara had been taken out of the situation room and sent to recovery. This is when he would be expected to make an appearance at the mediunit if at all. He got up and forced himself to move slowly over to the building next door. This time, his walk over was a very different one from that morning. Kara was alive and the thought made him happier than he felt he had a right to be. As he came down the corridor looking for her room, he met her doctor.

"Ah Captain Ursin, it is good to see you." It was Dr. Dasiv Quiste. "I was not sure you were going to come."

"I did not think it necessary to be here until now," Logan replied coolly. "I understand my property tried to take her life?"

He could see Jason hovering anxiously in the background but he did not have to fear. Logan was in complete control and was not likely to give himself away.

"She almost succeeded. Another few minutes and you would have been visiting her in a disposal bag." Logan's blood ran cold at the doctor's words delivered without feeling. "But we managed to save and stabilize her."

"What is her status now?" Logan asked as casually as he could.

"She is expected to have a full recovery and should remain here for a day or two. But we will try to send her back as soon as possible." The doctor smiled knowingly, immediately setting Logan's teeth on edge.

"That would be greatly appreciated doctor," Logan said trying to keep the relief out of his voice.

"Even so Captain, she should not be subjected to any strenuous activities for a few days if you intend on keeping her around for a while," he said, looking meaningfully at Logan.

"I will take that under advisement doctor."

The doctor was not finished yet. "She arrived with her clothes torn and she also had access to a naked blade. Are you planning on keeping her?"

Logan was perturbed by the pointed question

65

and became cautious with his response. "Why do you ask?"

The doctor appeared slightly uncomfortable. "Due to her condition I was hoping that she was just of passing interest to you."

"And if she is?" Logan prompted, curious now as to where the conversation was going.

"Then I would be more than happy to take her off your hands before you feel the need to get rid of her or send her to the Kat House."

Logan felt fear course though his body. The Kat House was the nickname the troops had already given to the dorm where the communal women were kept. Logan could not help the stiffening of his jaw. Behind the doctor he saw the warning look Jason gave him, but he composed himself easily. "Are you asking for yourself doctor, or did you have someone else in mind?"

"Well she certainly looks like she could be a hell of a ride," he said with an unsavory smile, "but since I hold no rank, I doubt that I will be able to hold on to her."

Dr. Quiste was referring to the rule that would allow an outranking officer to claim another's sexual property. Somehow Logan did not think that such a law would stop the doctor from getting exactly what he wanted.

He knew that like him, Quiste also held a privileged position with the general. That fact alone granted him tremendous power. He decided that the doctor did not have an interest in Kara personally but was looking to acquire her for someone else.

Logan suddenly felt sure that he did not even want to pursue the conversation any further. "I will keep that in mind for the future doctor but I have only managed one night with my property so far. And now you are telling me that I will need to wait even longer before I can enjoy her again. So it might be a while before I am ready to pass her along."

"Of course," Dr. Quiste said with a forced smile. There was a slight pause but he showed no signs of moving on.

"May I see her?" Logan asked, trying for nonchalance again.

"You are welcome to, but she is still unconscious and is not likely to come around for another few hours. I am sure you will not need to spend any additional time here. If you have use of your adjunct, he too can leave without a problem. We can always contact him or you once she is ready to leave the mediunit."

"I appreciate the offer doctor but now that we have things well in hand, I would feel better if my man stayed here. Ideally, if you have no objections, it would be best if he remained right in the room while she is recovering. She came upon the blade quite by accident but she did not hesitate to use it. I would not want a recurrence of her trying to take her life with the first thing she could lay her hands on."

"Yes of course," said the doctor. "We could keep her restrained, but if you feel it the best use of your adjunct's time he is welcomed to stay."

Before Logan could respond to the offhanded comment the doctor continued. "Now if you will excuse me there are some pressing matters that I must attend to." He inclined his head stiffly to Logan, indicating that their little discussion was over.

"Of course," Logan said, stepping aside to let

Quiste proceed down the corridor. He exchanged a telling glance with Jason before he walked passed him and entered the room where Kara lay. He stopped short completely unprepared for the sight.

Kara looked so pale and delicate in her repose that she appeared ethereal. A nutribag hooked up to her by a tube, provided the nourishment and other medications that she needed. There was just a thin bandage wrapped around her injured wrist belying the fact that she had almost died from the wound it hid.

Logan's heart melted at the sight of her. He felt a strong urge to gather her in his arms and try to kiss her awake. Instead, he sat quietly by her side not daring to touch her. The door to the room was still ajar and she was sharing the space with another patient. A very competent looking nurse was bustling in and out, but Logan felt sure that she was observing everything closely. One false move would put both him and Kara in danger.

He looked at her for a short while marveling at her beauty and her smooth flawless complexion. Somehow it was hard to connect the almost elfin form that lay unconscious on the bed to the passionate, vibrant woman who had let him make love to her repeatedly last night. He knew he was right when he told the doctor that he was not yet through with this woman but in that moment he wondered if the day would ever come when that would be the case.

As much as he wanted to sit by her side for hours, propriety would only allow him a few minutes before he would arouse suspicion. He took his leave before long commissioning Jason to stay with her, but he needed no convincing. He felt only relief that he would not have to leave Kara's side.

It would be noticed and frowned upon if Logan should come back to visit Kara at the mediunit again - especially since he was leaving his personal aid there, so he charged Jason to return Kara to him as soon as possible.

Chapter 13

Kara awoke to the smell of medicines permeating the air. She was puzzled to find herself in a bed, hooked up to a nutribag. There was a burning sensation at her left wrist and suddenly the memory of what had happened came flooding back to her.

She was alive? She could hardly believe it. Joy and relief washed over her. What had she been thinking? Embarrassment coloured her face when she remembered what she had done. Recalling her feeling of intense regret while her blood was draining out of her she had thought that she would never see Logan again.

She looked around and saw that it was dark outside. Someone sat dozing on a chair near the door. Sadly it was not Logan but the man who had kept track of her on the field, and stood guard at her prison door.

As Kara observed him more closely, she became aware that he could not be more than a year or two older than she was. He slept with his head slumped to one side on his chest and she could not help but compare him to Logan. He was also very handsome but his features were boyish, while Logan was more of a sexy, sensual man.

Before seeing Logan and feeling as if she had been struck by lightning, it was someone like this man who would have appealed to her. In her experience, there were too many women who were into darkly, handsome men like Logan and Kara never felt like she wanted to compete for a man. After the night she had spent as his captive however, she was clear that she no longer felt, or thought like her former self.

Looking around the room again Kara wondered where she was and how she had gotten there. She had no concept of how much time had passed since she had blacked out. So far she had been falling unconscious and waking up in a different place each time. She found it very disorienting but she quickly got her bearings and saw that here was a golden opportunity to slip past her guard and gain her freedom.

She checked to see what was holding her to the bed and was delighted to discover that she was not restrained. If only she could disconnect the nutribag, she would be able to walk right out the door. Kara looked over at the man again and almost physically jumped to see him wide awake and regarding her closely. She could tell that he knew exactly what she was thinking and she looked away quickly. Without a word to her, he got up and left the room only to return a moment later with a nurse in tow.

The nurse appeared quite competent as she bustled about, checking Kara's vitals and making sure that everything was in order. She kept firing off questions at her concerning how she felt, and Kara kept her answers concise.

The man had vacated the room while she was being examined, but once the nurse left, he slipped back inside and sat wordlessly on the chair again. He had returned with what looked like a newspaper. Once he sat down, he promptly ignored her, turning his attention instead to the document in hand. It was unusual for her to see the actual physical copy of a paper instead of the portable Data Analyzer device that everyone used for their information.

Unfortunately for him, Kara was wide awake. She stared at the young man openly but he refused to acknowledge her. It was clear that he was very aware of her gaze because he had gone crimson in the face under her scrutiny. She was both amazed and amused by this. This young man looked so adolescent that it was hard to believe he was a part of the destruction that had crippled Mindalea.

"What are you reading?" she asked.

Jason looked up at her surprised that this was the first question that she would ask after regaining consciousness. The fact that she had asked it so conversationally as if they were old acquaintances was even more amazing.

He said nothing at first but when he saw that she was patiently waiting for an answer, he replied: "Nothing that would interest you. It is just a report on what occurred yesterday."

"You mean with the invasion?" she asked quietly. He nodded. "I guess you can't share any of that information with me then?" He shook his head.

The room was now private as the other occupant had been discharged earlier in the day and the door leading to the corridor was closed.

Kara requested that he sit closer to her because she felt that she needed to shout across the room to him. "I don't think that I want that stern nurse to return and chide me for being too loud."

Jason saw that she was teasing him but he got up reluctantly and dragged his chair a little closer to the bed before he sat down again.

"Closer," she demanded, and he got up immediately to obey. This brought a small smile to Kara's face and embarrassment again to his, but he moved his chair obediently and sat next to her.

"You obeyed me as if I just issued a command to you," Kara said. "Do you have to follow all of my orders?" The smile on her face turned slightly mischievous and there was a twinkle in her eyes that Jason had not missed.

It made him grind out his reply. "Only the ones that suit me," he said, looking at her with menace.

"So I can have you to bring me a glass of water but not to set me free."

"Something like that," he replied as if she was pulling the words from him reluctantly.

"Is that a direct order from Logan?"

"Yes."

"Where is he anyway? Has he already replaced me with another?" She asked it flippantly but she found herself waiting anxiously for his reply.

"I wouldn't know," he replied through clenched teeth.

"I would be very upset too if I were you," Kara said sweetly after a short silence. "He gets to enjoy all the pleasures he can lay his hands on while you get to play nursemaid to me. It does not sound like a very glorious assignment for someone who has just conquered the great nation of Mindalea. Does it?"

He remained silent, deciding that it was not even worth the trouble to answer that particular question. Seeing that she was not going to get anywhere with him this way, Kara tried again. "What is your name?" He remained silent, focusing on the words before him. "Aren't you supposed to co-operate with me and minimize my undue stress?" she asked, blinking her large dark eyes at him innocently.

He looked up at her wondering where she meant to take the conversation, but he still did not respond. "Well, are you?"

He sighed noticeably and made a big show of putting the paper down on the side table.

"What would you have of me?" he asked in a voice full of exasperation, as if speaking to a child who was bothering him.

"I would have your name," she said just as formally but it was clear that she was trying to suppress a smile. Jason was caught off guard but taken by her playfulness. He marveled that this woman could slit her wrist one moment and behave as if nothing had happened in the next.

"Jason Sivirt," he said simply and more patiently.

"Really?" she asked in mock surprise. "Not mighty conqueror or: The Great Jason Sivirt?" Jason looked at her a bit sheepishly with a slight lopsided smile but said nothing.

"I just thought you would have a mighty sounding name if you had just managed to conquer the world."

As she continued to tease him he felt like he needed to retaliate. "I did just tell you that my compliance is up to my discretion right?" She nodded cautiously.

"Well, I also have authority over you and one of the things I can do is bound and gag you so that you shut up." His words had the desired effect he wanted. The fear of being restrained and silenced showed clearly in her expressive eyes before she was able to hide it behind a face full of bravado. She said nothing more and he returned to his report with a smug smile.

Kara stayed quiet for a full five minutes before she felt the need to speak again. "Is Logan angry with me?" she asked, timidly.

So finally she had brought it up, Jason thought. He raised his head from his reading and scrutinized her fully. She looked so frail and vulnerable that he had to resist the urge to join her on the narrow bed and gather her in his arms.

After a moment where she could actually see a war raging inside him as to what he should do, he finally sighed in earnest and put the paper to the side of him for good.

"No, he is not angry with you."

"Then why isn't he here."

"He cannot be here," Jason replied quietly.

"I don't understand."

Jason hesitated for a moment as he fought the urge to reach over and gently smooth away the frown on her beautiful brow. "Suffice it to say that he wants you to recover and come back to him as soon as possible but that he is not able to come to you," he said solemnly.

He did not mention that Logan had already been there twice already. Moved to see Kara look so anxious, Jason was curious to know if she wanted to return to Logan. "Do you want to get out of here as soon as possible?" he asked instead. She nodded. "Then get some rest so that we can convince these people to let you out of here."

Kara did not miss the 'us' as opposed to the 'you' and felt comforted, despite the fact that the man who sat there was her enemy. She remembered what Logan had said about there being many eyes and ears at Straveng, so even though she wanted to ask Jason a number of other things she thought it best to wait. She was suddenly feeling quite tired again and within minutes she was fast asleep.

Jason could not help but feel wonder at how easily she had given in to him and then fallen asleep like a child. He did not move his chair back to its original position but try as he might to concentrate on the paper which he had picked up again, his eyes kept straying to Kara.

Even though she had fallen asleep facing away from him, she tossed her head in her restless sleep and her face was now turned towards him. He could not help himself. He stared at her openly, aching to reach out and touch her cheek and to run the tip of his finger over her full, sensual lips, but he did not dare. Instead, he allowed his eyes to caress every inch of her beautiful face now that he was able to see it so close up and for such a long time.

He had spent a lot of time following her but being able to watch her while she slept was a special treat. He soaked up the sight of her in repose aware that he might never have an opportunity to do so again.

When his PI pinged softly Jason jumped guiltily as if he had been caught with his hand in the cookie jar. It was almost two hours since they had last communicated about Kara, and since it was well after midnight, he had assumed that Logan had given in to exhaustion and fallen asleep.

He was glad to be able to report that Kara had awoken for a bit and spoken a little before falling back asleep. Jason hoped the information would suffice for his captain to finally get some much needed rest.

Before signing off for the night, Logan reiterated that he needed Jason to ensure that Kara was brought back to him as soon as possible. "Naturally I am expecting you both later today," his final message read.

Chapter 14

The same nurse who had been attending to Kara since she had left the situation room on the previous day arrived the next morning to check her vitals. She managed to startle Jason awake and he could not help wondering how long the woman's shift really lasted - she seemed to be there forever. He suspected that it was likely she was working extra hours because the captain's property was in her care.

"You should go get some rest." she said, looking at him disapprovingly. "This one can hardly escape even if she tried."

"I know," Jason said, "but my orders are to stay with her until she is discharged."

"Well for your sake I will see what I can do," said the nurse, as Kara stirred and woke up. "If her vitals check out, I don't see any reason why she could not leave by mid-day."

Jason perked up when he heard this. He gave the nurse a dazzling smile as if she had just made his day.

"That would be great," he said.

She smiled tightly back at him and continued looking at him pointedly. He returned her gaze perplexed until it finally dawned on him what was required. He had gotten so comfortable sitting by Kara that he forgot he was in the habit of providing her some privacy when the nurse came to tend to her needs.

He sprung from the chair so quickly that the nurse could not help but turn her head to hide a genuine smile of amusement. With his face colouring, he mumbled something about being right outside if he was needed and left the room abruptly.

Kara lay docilely on the bed, allowing the nurse to take her temperature and check her vitals. She answered her questions politely but concisely. Once she had finished doing what was required, Nurse Eva Juell became a little more relaxed and conversational.

Juell worked closely with Doctor Quiste which meant that she was often privy to his conversations with the general. If there was some intelligence to be gleaned from this episode concerning Captain Ursin she was going to try to ferret it out.

Specifically, she wanted to know why Kara had tried to take her life after only one night with the man. The captain was well known and liked on the base - especially by a number of the women. Since Juell worked with many of them, she was naturally curious about the prize that Logan had claimed for his own.

There were no signs that the woman had been forced or hurt in anyway, except of course for the minor telltale marks on her wrists yesterday. Even so, those only indicated that she had been restrained for a short while at one point or another. This was hardly unusual given the circumstances.

Juell felt sure that captive or not, Captain Ursin would still be hard to resist. So what had happened? As much as she wanted to question the woman out right about it she could not risk having her tell the captain about their conversation. Her direct inquiry would be seen as being out of line and could come with consequences.

"Your vitals look fine so there is a good chance you will be discharged today," she said, instead. "Would you like that?" Juell acted friendly, but was observing Kara closely.

"Yes, of course," she replied simply.

Juell persisted. "You do realize that the man who is with you is waiting to take you back to the captain right?" she asked, resting her gaze pointedly on Kara's injured wrist.

Jason, who stood right outside the door so that he could be privy to just such a conversation wondered if he should re-enter the room, but knew his action was likely to arouse suspicion. Instead, he stood by and held his breath. He felt sure that the nurse was baiting Kara and he wondered if she would take it.

"I know," Kara said, "but this has been my fault. It will not happen again." Jason breathed a sigh of relief. His good opinion of the woman was growing by leaps and bounds.

"That is good to hear," the nurse said in her tight voice.

Kara too, instinctively felt that the nurse was trying to trap her. She had no doubts that she was sitting in the middle of a hornets' nest. No matter how helpful someone appeared to be they could not be trusted. If she betrayed Logan in any way, it was likely that she could end up in a far worse position. Better the devil you know than the one you didn't, she thought.

There was a long pause as if Juell was giving Kara an opportunity to renege on her response, but she remained silent "What contraceptive are you on?" Neither Kara nor Jason was expecting that question. She blushed deeply but said nothing.

Juell's eyebrows shot up in surprise. "Are you even on a contraceptive?" she asked, unable to prevent the contempt in her voice. Kara shook her head, completely red in the face. "You know that is both irresponsible and fool hardy of you, don't you?" This time the nurse was not even bothering to hide her disdain.

In truth, Kara had not even thought about it. The discussion having suddenly been raised it was enough to cause the alarm bells to go off madly in her head. She'd had sex with Logan repeatedly during their night together and she had not once thought about protection. She felt both self-disgust and anger because neither had he.

Jason stood in agony for her outside the door. He could not imagine what she must be going through. If she had not been sexually active before there was likely no need for a contraceptive. But the nurse did not know that she had been a virgin before she spent the night with Logan.

Kara was silent on the subject and Jason was both relieved and admiring that she had not taken the bait and tried to justify her situation in the face of such disapproval. He wondered how much longer she would need to endure the nurse's interrogation.

"I will make sure that the doctor prescribes something for you," the nurse continued. "Thankfully you were only with the captain one night, but you should not continue to take chances. Do you have a preference for something?" There was silence from where Jason stood but Kara must have indicated something because the nurse said: "Then I will leave it up to the doctor to decide." With that she left, nodding briefly at Jason as she walked by.

When he came back into the room Jason exchanged a long, solemn look with Kara that spoke volumes between them. She had no doubts that he had heard the entire conversation. As much as it was mortifying, it also made her feel safer knowing that Jason was not planning to leave her side.

Chapter 15

A change of clothing had been delivered to the mediunit for a relieved Kara. None of her things had been returned to her so she was dreading having to leave the building in just the medigown and no underclothes.

Dr Quiste arrived shortly after mid-day to discharge her. Before he left, he gave her a small vial of pills, "I suggest you get started on these right away." It was the contraceptive.

Turning to Jason he addressed him as if Kara was not even there. "She is still weak and should be kept here for at least another day but I am sure you are anxious to return to your regular duties. Tell the captain that he needs to allow for at least seventy-two hours of rest before he resumes intimacy," he said, before leaving the room.

Jason could not help the colour that rose to his face, and neither could Kara. He did not look at her directly as he muttered something about her changing her clothes before he left the room.

She did so as quickly as she could just as keen as he was to leave the place. But even putting on clothes had suddenly become a strenuous activity for her. When she was finished, she sat on the bed feeling fatigued but impatient for Jason to reappear.

Thankfully, he knocked at the door and came in before long. Walking up to her, he reached down to scoop her up from the bed. "What are you doing?" she exclaimed in alarm. "I can walk just fine, thank you."

She looked completely affronted so Jason was about to explain that he was under explicit orders to take her bodily back but he decided wisely against saying anything about that last message he had received from Logan. He did not challenge her but he stayed right by her side as she walked out of the room with her head held high.

By the time they had made their way out of the building, Kara was already feeling dizzy. Swaying suddenly she would have fallen had Jason not been there to catch her neatly. He lifted her easily into his arms while Kara blushed to the roots of her hair, but she did not struggle as he walked with her towards the very next building.

At first Jason started off at a smart pace, carrying her like she weighed no more than a feather, but as he neared the Brock building he unconsciously slowed his pace. It felt so good to hold her that he wanted to prolong the moment. He could not say that carrying her in his arms was another first but this time it felt so different.

He recalled his trek across the campus only too well just yesterday when his whole being was focused on ensuring she lived. Today she was alive and vibrant in his arms and he wanted to savor the feeling.

"Is that where you are taking me?" she asked, gesturing towards the Brock Building.

He nodded. "You have been occupying a room in the basement. The captain works on the sixth floor."

"There are no windows in that room," Kara said sadly. Jason did not respond. "Please don't take me in there just yet," she blurted out.

Her plea cut Jason's heart to the quick. This girl was a complete innocent who had unwittingly become a prisoner of war as had many other Mindaleans in similar circumstances. They had been caught completely unaware and had suffered for it.

For the first time since the invasion the outcome and the aftermath of his people's actions filtered through his conscience in a different way. He saw her as a victim rather than the enemy that had condemned his people to a life of exile on the small island of Rhinaris as he was led to believe.

He was happy on some level to spend more time out in the open with her because soon enough they would both be cooped up for long periods of time in a windowless basement. Still, he felt it his duty to insist. "You are quite weak. We should get you something more substantial to eat as soon as possible."

"Yes we should," Kara agreed earnestly," and I promise I will eat everything that is set before me – just, not right now."

A bench conveniently appeared close by so he sat her down on it and took the seat next to her. People were walking to and fro, some in a hurry, others throwing curious glances at them as she sat with her face upturned to catch the rays of sunlight.

It was a beautiful day, with the sun peeping through the leaves of the trees its rays dancing on the ground. Under different circumstances it would have seemed perfect to sit there with someone like her, Jason thought. But she belonged to another man; one he highly respected and could not hope to contend with, challenge or disobey in any way.

The thought was enough to sober him. "We should go," he said, after only a short while.

Kara knew from the change in the tone of his voice that the moment was over. Without protesting, she got up from the bench. "I'd like to walk from here if you don't mind Jason," she announced.

He would remember the way she said his name

for a long time to come, replaying it over and over in his head while he savored the sound. He was not sure that she could manage the feat on her own but she had conceded to his request so willingly that it seemed only fair for him to do likewise.

Chapter 16

Kara walked into the building steadily enough, her eyes darting everywhere. She would not have been able to enter the lobby just a few days ago because the whole building was zoned as a construction site. Of course that all changed with the invasion when there was the sudden realization that the building was fully functional. The scaffolding was pulled down and all other signs of heavy construction were removed to reveal a magnificent structure.

They needed to get through only a single checkpoint before they were able to access the bank of elevators in the lobby. There was no down button on any of the elevators that Kara could see, Jason however, did not take her to any of them. Instead, he walked past them all, directing her down a quiet corridor where there was only one additional elevator. He pressed the single button that did not indicate a particular direction on it. When the door opened and they stepped into it by themselves, he produced a key and inserted it in one of the slots to access a particular floor.

The elevator dropped quickly so Kara was puzzled at how long it still took before it finally stopped. She was curious to ask Jason if there were multiple levels beneath the building but instinctively she felt it was not the place to do so. Many elevators in public areas were likely to have recording lenses. As he led her down a long, dimly lit corridor, Kara could see that she was right. A number of them were discreetly placed at intervals indicating that recording coverage continued.

Eventually Jason opened a door and Kara was once again standing on the threshold of the room that had recently become both her prison and her paradise.

As she entered, she could not help but feel a slight dread at how quiet it seemed. She was not looking forward to spending long hours in the room by herself but the feeling did not overwhelm her relief at being alive in the first place.

There was a large bouquet of flowers on the night stand with a card from Logan welcoming her back. There was also a full spread of food awaiting them for lunch on the table.

Jason's PI pinged softly and he flipped it open. "The captain is hoping to join you for lunch," he said, after glancing at the screen.

"He is?" she blurted out in surprise.

Jason nodded. "He is trying to get out of the office to make his way down to you as we speak."

Did she actually feel a thrill at this announcement? Yes. She would be happy to see him again. She also felt a little embarrassed about her actions and wondered if she would be shy with him. Kara moved towards the bathroom and the memories of what had happened only yesterday immediately assailed her.

The door had been removed and replaced with a thick curtain. She guessed they were not prepared to take any more chances. She stood in front of the mirror and looked at a face that appeared pale and haunted.

Out of curiosity she opened the mirrored door above the sink. It was now completely empty and there were only the basics like soap, shampoo, towels and toilet paper in the little room.

She took her time freshening up, trying her best to make herself presentable. Jason called out to her before sticking a hand through the curtain holding a hair brush. "I thought you might want this," he said, and she took it gratefully, unable to suppress a smile.

"Thanks," she said softly.

"You're welcome," he murmured from behind the curtain.

By the time she had re-emerged from the bathroom, Jason's face was solemn. "The captain will not be able to join you after all."

Kara's heart sank but she tried not to show her disappointment. Jason was not fooled. "He is very disappointed that he could not come, but he will join you as soon as he can."

Kara was impressed with Jason. He took his opportunities to defend Logan at every turn even when it was clear that he was attracted to her himself.

"Kara you must eat," he said, pulling out a chair for her to sit. It was the first time she'd heard him call her by name. She liked hearing it so much that she decided not to bring it to his attention, or to tease him about it.

Since she had promised him that she was not going to put up a fight about eating, she promptly sat down. She had also said that she was going to eat everything that was laid before her as well but currently the table held more food than she could manage. "Will you join me?" It had not taken long for her to become comfortable with Jason and she could tell that he felt the same about her.

Jason was glad that she had asked. Besides being completely famished he could not think of anywhere else he'd rather be. Logan had messaged suggesting he stay and have lunch with her. He had also been instructed not to leave her alone in the room under any circumstances but Jason was not going to insist on eating with her as well if it made her uncomfortable. "Yes," he said, "I think I will. Thank you."

As he sat down, she asked him about the building they were in and what Logan did. He was free with his responses compared to his reluctance to talk the previous day. He saw no reason to keep the information from her now that they were stowed away in the basement. He knew that she was just trying to making sense of what had become of her world.

The building was huge and supposedly a research facility, but it actually housed a piece of technology called the Dunlop Dampener or DD. The device was even now projecting a signal that disabled function cubes in almost all forms of Mindalean technology. None of it could work once the signal was turned on, and Kara was sure that this was the weakness that Logan had alluded to a couple of nights before.

Unfortunately, the Mindaleans had opted for the ease of creating almost all their technology using function cubes. The machine part was standardized using the same components and operated similarly from one device to the other. "Your people never anticipated that their lives could be hijacked in this manner, rendering all their electronic tools, appliances, mobiles and gadgets as useless. We have been working on the technology for years and only recently perfected it," Jason explained frankly.

The pulse needed to be amplified by strategically placed DDs within Mindalea that would ensure simultaneous coverage over the entire nation. Straveng was one such site where the projector was being built in secret while the building was under construction. Once Mindalean technology was disabled the Giddians used the element of surprise to quickly overwhelm their enemy's defenses.

"Logan's mother and father were the primary leaders who worked on the DD project. From an early age, Logan was groomed to succeed them. He not only learned quickly from them but he was able to competently build upon their success," Jason said proudly. "Despite being so young he now remains the foremost expert on the technology we used to defeat your people." He seemed to realize too late that he was being insensitive and looked embarrassed but Kara just sat, stunned by the information.

"That was how we managed the invasion and defeat of Mindalea with such ease," he continued, choosing his words more carefully. "We disabled everything and then attacked."

Kara felt a hard knot in her stomach when she thought of the key role Logan had played in the downfall of her people. "But I saw air mobiles" she argued. "I knew they were not ours so they must have been yours. Wouldn't the DD affect your technology as well?"

Jason smiled sadly. "Knocking out your technology was only part of a well thought out plan. In preparation for the attack we have been trained on weaponry and technology that does not depend on function cubes. Our equipment and a number of our mobiles were unaffected by the signal from the projector. We revisited the technology that existed prior to the function cube to create our current weapons and machines. That is also why you were able to access a manual razor in the bathroom. No Mindalean electronics currently work."

Kara was blown away. She ate quietly while she tried to absorb this information. Compared to the

Mindaleans, the Giddians were seen as a very small nation of people that lagged behind Mindalea in every way. Yet now it was plain to see that her people's biggest mistake was not building their lives on function cubes but underestimating the Giddians.

Jason also stayed quiet as he ate. He watched her overtly as the cogs turned in her mind. Since Jason was being so accommodating and Kara did not know when he was likely to be so again, she wanted to know more. "Who is the leader of the Giddian people?"

Jason answered without hesitation. "A brilliant man named General Atto Degan; he was there on the sports field."

Kara could not help the chill that ran through her. She recalled the tall, thin-faced man who had stood on the stage and addressed the crowd that day.

"I remember," she said softly, in awe that she had not stood far from the man who ordered the attack on her people.

"In the twenty years that he has led our people, he has managed to further our cause more than any other leader in recent times. He continued to send people purposefully to Mindalea, like his predecessor, all with very specific objectives that eventually culminated into this attack."

Kara was incredulous. "You are saying that thousands of Giddian refugees were planted here?"

Jason nodded. "General Degan commands the utmost respect among my people. His influence has been stronger than any Mindalean enticement."

Kara thought about this for a while. Her people had opened their arms to the Giddian refugees, assuming that they were saving them from some warped, socialistic regime. Their politicians even advocated for the best homes, schools and jobs for qualified refugees. It had not taken long for many to climb to prominence within their society. Mindaleans themselves no longer made a distinction between its own citizens and those they welcomed with open arms.

Kara felt betrayed and defeated at the same time. She was well aware that the arrogance of her people had done more to cause their downfall than anything the Giddians could have done. "What will become of my people now?" she asked dejectedly.

Jason stayed quiet; almost as if he had been dreading that particular question all along. She remained silent herself; not wanting to let him off the hook. It was obvious that he had heard her, so she just waited with bated breath for his reply.

"We see your people differently from how you see ours," he started slowly. "Mindalea was initially a place for Giddians who could not work as part of the whole, to escape to. Here they could become individuals and practice capitalism," he said in a slightly scornful tone. "Mindalea turned its back on Giddia a long time ago. It condemned and corralled my people on a small island while it sprawled itself over the rest of the land, draining and misusing its natural resources."

He spoke with passion and conviction but Kara wondered how much of what he was saying came directly from him and how much of it was propaganda.

"At first it was only talk about what would happen if we ever were to conquer Mindalea. But as talk brought on the possibility of reality, consensus built and laws were created to govern the invasion. Any Mindalean who was captured would become the property of Giddia." Jason paused and looked at Kara directly with his intense eyes.

Kara just sat uncomprehending. She had heard the term "property" thrown around a bit at the mediunit and Logan had talked about her belonging to him but she had paid very little attention to the terminology before. Suddenly understanding dawned on her causing her, to open her eyes wide. "You mean like slaves?" she asked incredulously.

Jason looked at her piercingly and replied simply: "Yes."

This was too much for Kara to take. She sprang up from the table. They had finished their meal but had stayed at the table talking. The true horror of her situation and that of every other Mindalean that was being held in captivity started to seep into her conscience. The majority of her people would be treated as captives, and held as prisoners of war.

"But how can they do that?" she asked, as she paced the room agitatedly. "Calling someone a slave does not necessarily make it so," she said in defiance.

Jason shrugged. "You saw what happened on the sports field with your own eyes Kara," he said firmly, as if willing her to wake up to the nightmare that was her reality. "And if you had slipped up just once at the mediunit, you would have been taken away from Captain Ursin and given to someone else who I assure you, would have made you really feel like taking your life. Still, such a fate might be more preferable than being assigned to the Kat House where you would become the property of every Giddian man who took a fancy to you." Kara stared at him in horror.

Jason who had been getting tense as he spoke, suddenly sighed in resignation. He was sorry for frightening her. He just wanted her to understand that no matter how bad she thought she had it with Logan, it would be a lot worse for her if she was not with him.

Kara had not missed Jason's motive, and she marveled at the man who could inspire such loyalty in someone who served under him. She sat down again meekly at the table. "Please do not stop. I want to know more. Tell me about your leader," she coaxed.

Jason looked at her closely to see if she was even capable of accepting more information before he continued. "Part of his brilliance is that he follows a strategy where we operate in pods. Often one pod does not know about the workings and goals of another. Captain Ursin and I, along with most of the people here were assigned to making sure that Brevika was secured, and that Straveng was converted into a base. That process is not yet complete and there is still much to be done."

"Like what?" Kara prompted, but this time it was Jason who got up from the table.

"I am not privy to that information myself," he said curtly, "and I suggest that you do not bring it up with the captain either. Much of what he does is considered classified. He could easily become compromised for sharing information with anyone and I am sure that neither you nor I would like that to happen."

Jason's meaning was clear even if mostly unspoken. Logan appeared to be her only shield against what was happening around her. Not even Jason could be considered an ally unless Logan wished it so. If she were to lose Logan in that capacity she would essentially be bringing about her own doom. Kara had already made one major mistake that had almost killed her. She was not prepared to do something again that could bring danger to them all.

"You should rest," said Jason. Even as he said it, Kara felt an overwhelming sense of fatigue. "I will stay with you until the captain arrives."

He walked over and drew the covers away from the bed to indicate that she should lie down. He could not help but glance down at the sheets below and even though he expected it he was still relieved to see that they had been replaced.

"How do you do that?" she asked in exasperation as she slid obediently under the sheets.

"How do I do what?" he asked, knitting his brow in puzzlement.

"How do you just say 'go to bed' and make me feel instantly like I should?"

As she got in he pulled up the covers gently and like a magnificent nursemaid, he tucked her in. "Maybe it is because I already feel like I know you too well," he said smiling easily. Kara said nothing in reply but she could not help thinking it might be true. Was she so easy to read?

She watched him take up a seat on a chair at the table and pull out some bended sheets of paper from his pocket to focus on. She marveled at the fact that she continued to feel strangely comforted by his presence in the room rather than standing guard outside the door.

As tired as she felt she did not think that sleep would come easily to her. Her mind felt like it was spinning with all the information that Jason had so willingly shared with her but within minutes she was fast asleep.

Chapter 17

Logan came in just as the supper cart arrived. Wheeling it in himself he was greeted with a smart salute from Jason but he quickly motioned for him to be at ease.

"You look like shit," Logan whispered as he smiled and shook Jason's hand. He held it in a firm handshake before releasing him.

"That is because my superior has me playing nursemaid without rest for the past forty-eight hours," Jason retorted with a grin.

"And for that I thank you," Logan said sincerely. He moved to the bed to observe Kara and was once again struck by her beauty in repose.

There were more than a couple of times during the first few hours after the incident when he thought he would never lay eyes on her alive again. He was anxious to be alone with her but first there was the need to debrief with Jason.

Logan motioned for Jason to step out of the room with him. "How is she?" he asked once they were in the corridor.

"Better than expected for what she has undergone," Jason replied.

Logan nodded soberly. "Has she been asleep long?"

"For a few hours. The doctor has ordered that you make no demands of her physically for at least seventy-two hours."

Logan only nodded as if he already expected that. "How did it go at the mediunit?" Jason went into the details of his time there often repeating information he had already passed along in his PI messages to the captain. Logan appreciated hearing a full account of what had happened again. When he got to the part about nurse Juell and her interrogation of Kara Logan listened carefully. He looked at Jason in wonder when he related how Kara sensing a trap, accepted full responsibility for what had happened rather than lay blame on him.

After Jason was through debriefing him, Logan rested his hand on his shoulder in a rare display of sincere affection and camaraderie. "You have done well my friend. Go now and get some well deserved rest. I would like you to report back here in the morning, and for you to do so every morning to be with Kara. I do not want her to be alone. But I can understand if you feel your time could be better spent elsewhere, and can make other arrangements."

"I will be here," Jason replied promptly, with a smile. "I know how important this is to you."

Logan looked instantly relieved. "Go then. Find someone to warm your bed tonight. I will see you before I leave in the morning." Jason nodded and wasted no time taking his leave.

He decided to take his captain's advice but after experiencing Kara up close and personal, he had no desire to be with an unwilling Mindalean woman at the Kat House. Instead, he thought it better to seek the embrace of one of his own kind. Taking out his PI as he walked away, he put in a call to Gracie Caraby who often entertained him.

As always, Gracie was glad for his company but on this occasion when he slept with her, in his mind's eye, it was a petite, dark haired Mindalean that he was making love to. It was no wonder that Gracie seemed a poor outlet for his lust that night and when he finally crawled into his own bed at one of the barracks Jason felt as if he was still hungering for something that stood just beyond his reach.

Despite feeling famished, Logan left the food untouched and drew his chair close to Kara instead. As he sat in the chair quietly looking at her, he wanted nothing more than to take her into his arms and just hold her, but he did not dare. He had no idea what to expect from her when next she awoke. After all, she had tried to take her own life on his account just yesterday.

He was not sure how long he sat there with his eyes fixed on her before she began rising out of a deep sleep. He could see that she was being troubled by some nightmare as she tossed her head from side to side and moaned softly. Despite her troubled sleep, she looked sexy and completely fuckable yet her body was off limits for three whole days according to the doctor's advice.

Just as he thought to wake her she cried out in her sleep and her eyes sprang open. She looked around wildly until her eyes settled on him. "Logan?" she asked. "Are you really here at last?" He could not have been more stunned by her question and her tone. It melted his heart.

He had expected a berating for selfishly taking her repeatedly. He had expected sullenness, even coldness, but he was not prepared for such a warm reception. Her eyes were tearing up, and she looked at him with regret. "I'm sorry," she said.

For what? he wondered in bewilderment as he crossed the divide between them and took her into his arms. He kissed her lips and all parts of her face, holding her tightly. "I thought I had lost you Kara," he whispered emotionally. His heart overflowed with joy when he felt her kissing him back as she clung to him desperately.

"I am so very sorry," she murmured again.

"For what? I am the one who should be apologizing to you. I did not realize that my selfish actions could cause you to try to take your life. I thought that you might hate me for pushing you to such a limit."

Kara shook her head and was crying tears of relief and happiness. She had missed this man. She remembered the intense feeling of panic and regret she had felt at never being able to see him again after she had slit her wrist. Yet here she was given a second chance to be with him. Somewhere along the line she had come to terms with the fact that it was better to have this man, if only for a little while than not at all.

"I should never have tried to take my life," she said. "I don't even know what came over me. I opened up the cabinet and the razor was just there. It felt like the easiest thing in the world to run it across my wrist. But from the moment I did it I felt regret that I would never see you again."

Logan was dumbstruck. Out of all that he felt could have pass between them he would have never guessed that she would be baring her very soul to him. He sat on the bed just holding her. He had been beating up on himself for being careless with the razor and yet out of that tragedy, his salvation was emerging like a phoenix.

When he did not say anything, she continued. "I had an awful dream just now. When I woke up, I realized that I was living my nightmare and yet I feel safe with you. You do not seem a part of all of this madness even though I know this to be untrue."

"Kara, I did the only thing I knew to do to protect you. I am sorry that I forced you, but it never entered my mind that you would willingly accept me. All I could think about was to possess you, body and soul."

"I know," she murmured, and there was such acceptance in those two words that Logan felt emotion well up in him like a surging tide. To help dispel the feeling, he tilted her head back and ravaged her mouth so thoroughly that at last she had to push against him as she gasped for breath.

"I should lie back down," she said. "I feel a little lightheaded."

He was quick to agree lying right beside her and taking her into his arms.

"You should have some supper," he said, after a short while where they were both silent. He was loath to disturb the bond and closeness they had developed in just minutes but ensuring that she ate had become a top priority for him.

"I should," she said, "and I have a promise to keep."

"A promise?" he asked her quizzically.

Kara raised her head to meet his eyes and she smiled. It completely took Logan's breath away. She was beautiful and he treasured her smile because it was given genuinely and selflessly.

He was touched immediately by a pang of deep regret. A glimpse of the life they might have had together if they had not been caught up in this mess, flashed before his eyes. He felt a moment of complete self loathing. Kara could not be blamed for what had brought them to this point; only he.

"I promised Jason that I would eat well without being forced, in exchange for __." She suddenly

99

stopped, unsure of whether she should continue.

"Yes?" he prompted when it appeared as if she was reluctant to go on.

She was caught between a rock and a hard place. She did not want to say anything to get Jason in trouble. Yet she felt that this was a new beginning between Logan and herself and she did not want to start it off by keeping secrets from him.

"In exchange for information," she mumbled sullenly. Her little girl manner was too much for him. A laugh that he tried to suppress started low in his abdomen and rumbled through him before exploding full force.

"I really don't know what to make of you," he said eventually when he saw the bewilderment on her face. "You go from hating the two of us, to professing your amorous feelings for me and protecting Jason in just a couple of days."

Kara blushed. "You make me sound fickle and traitorous to my own people," she said petulantly. "I guess I just had to come to terms with the fact that I am sleeping with my enemy," she continued more lightly, intending for it to be a joke. The expression however made Logan solemn. Kara was indeed sleeping with the enemy he thought and there was no way for both their sakes that he should ever forget that.

She saw the sudden change on his face at her words and she lifted herself up on her elbow to face him as he lay against the pillows. She marveled at his chiseled features and wanted to reach out and trace the lines of his lips, chin and nose, but it was clear that he had become morose. Her curiosity burned at the sudden change in him. "What is it?"

He shook his head. "It's nothing," he said trying

to take her back into his arms so that she could help to dispel the dark thoughts that had started to crowd into his head.

She persisted. "No," she said, gently resisting him. "Please tell me."

He looked at her for a long moment. When he saw that she was likely to prove stubborn about the matter, he sighed in an exaggerated manner. "Your words have managed to bring back the reality of our situation to me," he said. "I am a lone man who is now committed to protecting my greatest treasure. But there are those who would try to take you away from me."

"But we are locked away here, and I am removed and sheltered," she persisted.

"Yes but not for long," Logan said seriously.

She rose up into a sitting position on the bed and looked down at him. "What do you mean?"

At first he said nothing, appearing as if he was trying to work out something in his head, but eventually he said: "Staying here was only meant to be temporary. The General has ensured a proper living space for the officers and their prop__, their partners," he finished.

She smiled at him sadly. "It was not partners you were initially going to say, was it?"

He looked at her searchingly. "No," he finally admitted.

"Jason told me that I am now considered your property." This time she looked down at the bed, unable to meet his eyes.

"Yes," he said quietly, "by Giddian law. And while I might have considered you as such just a short while ago, it is not how I see you now."

Kara waited for him to continue. He raised himself up on one elbow so that he could tilt her head to look at him directly. "I know now, that you are my life partner and I will never be able to see you as anything else." His words sent a thrill through her. What he said felt so completely right that she reached down and kissed him reassuringly.

He engulfed her in his arms drawing her closer to him so that he could deepen the kiss, making her sigh with contentment. "I wish I could make love to you Kara," he murmured with regret, as they finally broke apart.

"Then why don't you?" she breathed sexily, nuzzling his neck. She knew well enough what the doctor had said but she felt sure that she could handle Logan physically and she wanted this as badly as he did.

He groaned. "I can't," he said. "You know that." He disengaged himself fully from her. He felt incapable of restraint under her bold onslaught of physical intimacy. He knew that only distance between their bodies would help now with his resolve.

"Come," he said, "you must eat." He got off the bed briskly. Taking her hand, he led her over to the supper cart. She offered no resistance as he directed her to choose what she wanted so that they could take their plates over to the small table.

"Have I gotten Jason into trouble?" she asked tentatively, as they sat down.

Logan seemed preoccupied. "Pardon?"

"I just wanted to know if Jason would get into trouble for sharing information with me."

He shook his head. "Not if that little fact stays between us," he said looking at her significantly.

The thought had bothered her for the past few minutes and she was relieved to know that she had not landed Jason in hot water. What Logan did not say was that Jason had already informed him of all he had told her during their debriefing.

Kara decided to return to the topic that they had left off while on the bed. "You said that we may have to move to new living quarters. What is it like? Will there be lots of natural light?"

Logan looked at her and his expression softened. He had continued to look distracted as if he was wrestling internally with something but when Kara said that she hoped there would be lots of light in their new place it was almost as if a decision had been made for him.

He took a deep breath. "Yes Kara, there will be lots of light because there are large windows." Her eyes lit up. "But don't get your hopes up in case you are thinking about trying anything silly again," he said smiling. "The construction crew took their time to ensure that bars have been securely placed over each window."

She looked at him with an exaggeratedly hurt expression as if to say: "How could you possibly think that I had escape on my mind?" And he grinned back at her.

"Compared to here, it would seem like a penthouse suite but there are draw backs as well."

When he did not elaborate she prompted. "Like what?"

"Well for one thing," he said reluctantly, "it is where the other officers will be staying so there will be the need for extra caution. Most of them will be treating their partners as possessions."

He paused as if completely unwilling to go on but since he knew she was likely to persist anyway, he continued. "The general has also made it possible for an officer of higher rank to claim the prize of another."

Kara looked at him in horror. "But that is barbaric!"

"And yet that is the reality of the situation," he countered crisply.

She understood the tone of his voice as an indicator that she should not pursue the topic. She felt her anger rising as well and wanted to ask him how he could ever buy into something like this. But it was clear that Logan was grappling with his thoughts and she did not want to upset the balance that currently existed between them. The damage had already been done and she felt as if she was on borrowed time. She certainly did not want to spend it arguing with this gorgeous man.

"It is easier to hide you away from the rest of the world here," Logan said, as if speaking to himself. "But if I do not join the rest of the officers eventually it will raise suspicion."

Kara was beginning to understand the dilemma Logan faced. If he continued to view her simply as property then there would be no dilemma about where to house her. "So what will we do?" she asked.

"I guess we will have to move into Drumlin Hall. At least that way you can have your light but you need to promise me that you will not ask to leave the apartment very often. Regularly there is only Alfred Grute who outranks me here on this base, but sometimes there are officers that are coming in from other pods. If you catch the eye of one of them, you could be taken away from me in a heartbeat."

Kara looked at Logan in horror. She was finally beginning to understand that she was constantly in grave danger. She was relieved that she "belonged" to

Logan and no other.

"Will you have no recourse if something like that happens?" Logan looked tortured as he shook his head. She felt like crying in self-pity and reaching for him across the table at the same time so that she could cradle him in her arms. The anguish and suffering in his eyes was almost unbearable. But instead of drawing attention to the topic she asked instead: "When would we have to go?"

"As early as tomorrow. The preparations were completed yesterday and since most of the officers only had temporarily accommodations, they were eager to take up residence in the building."

They were both silent for a while as they contemplated what this would mean for them both. Kara decided to change the topic entirely as she thought that it was too easy for them to slip into a dark mood.

"I was disappointed that you had not come down to lunch today." Logan had finished his supper and so had she.

"I was too," he said, taking a final drink of his wine. He got up and moving to her side he gathered her easily into his arms and walked back to the bed with her.

"You have no idea of the kind of hell I have lived in since you have been away," he said, laying her gently on the bed. "When I was required urgently just as I was heading for the elevator to join you I almost told Alfred to fuck off but I am now ever conscious of not drawing attention to myself on your account. I doubt I will be able to manage it for much longer now that we are required to go to the officers' quarters but I am desperate to keep you as safe as I can."

Kara reached up and kissed him again, long and

deeply as they groped each other gently. "We will do something tomorrow about expanding your wardrobe," he said with a grin, when they finally broke apart. She shrugged and he kissed her on the nose. "But for tonight," he continued, "it is time for both of us to get some sleep. Am I going to have to bind you to the bed Kara?" he asked half jokingly.

She shook her head vigorously. "No," she said. "Not after all of your horror stories about bad men wanting to take me away from you."

"Good," he said with self satisfaction, settling down with her in a close embrace.

Chapter 18

Kara awoke once again to the sound of running water in the bathroom. Within minutes, Logan emerged stark naked. He seemed unabashed while her heart quickened at the sight of him. As he walked towards the bed with his tousled hair, he looked tall, well built and so scrumptious that she suddenly felt intensely shy even though she had already been intimate with him.

At the sight of her still half asleep on the bed, his cock started to harden. It memorized Kara and filled her with longing. He knelt beside the bed and scooped her into his arms, but made no attempt to get in with her.

"Good morning," he said, kissing her immediately and deeply without waiting for a reply. Kara stiffened a little becoming immediately self-conscious about having morning breath.

She heard the soft rumble of his laugh deep inside him before it trickled out as a chuckle. "You need not worry about your breath Kara. It will always be sweet to me." He kissed her again just as deeply. This time she relaxed into his embrace and reached up to hold his head so that she could feel more of him. She wanted to entice him to stay and make love to her despite what the damn doctor had said.

Logan groaned and eventually broke the kiss, but she was gratified to see the fever raging in his eyes. "I have to go," he said as if he was trying to convince himself. "Jason will help you to move over to our new quarters today. But I'm afraid I will not see you until close to supper time. He will keep you company and ensure that you want for nothing but you should not press him to leave the apartment for any reason. Okay?"

Her heart sank at his words and the danger they seemed to imply. She nodded docilely.

He kissed her once more and got up briskly as if with a gargantuan effort. He was fully erect and she continued to boldly admire him. He smiled appreciatively at her open scrutiny.

"I hope you like what you see Miss Brinner," he said, twitching his beautiful specimen of manhood once for emphasis. His smile transformed into an all out grin when he saw her dark eyes open even wider. "Because I sure do like what I see. And I can't wait until I can have it all."

His words sent a thrill through her body, making her suddenly very hot. She was finding it difficult to breathe but Logan relished every minute he spent teasing her. With a self-satisfied smirk he pulled on his clothes slowly and almost seductively for her benefit. He laughed happily when she unconsciously licked her lips as she watched him enjoying the fact that she was as worked up as he felt. The sound of his uninhibited laughter made the butterflies in her stomach go crazy. Almost giving in to temptation, she wanted to beg him to ignore all the warnings and just fuck her mercilessly. Suddenly quite alarmed at her dirty thoughts she was embarrassed by the things this man was able to make her think and feel.

With one more kiss he left her hot and bothered on the bed before walking out the door. Kara felt as if Logan had completely set her up because Jason was already there to trade places with him before she could fully recover. She worked hard at composing herself, determined to not let Logan get the better of her.

Jason entered with the breakfast cart and a package which he placed on the bottom of the bed.

"Good morning," he said quietly. Kara responded in kind as if she was completely calm and composed.

He tried to casually scrutinize the supper cart as he wheeled it out causing Kara to smile. His behavior was effectively distracting her from her carnal thoughts.

When he walked back into the room he sat on a chair near the door and immediately produced a sheaf of papers to pore over. He did not raise his head for a while, even though she lay in bed and just stared at him.

Jason looked fresh, clean shaven and well rested. She wondered how long it would be before he started to become uncomfortable under her gaze and had to smile again when she saw the color rise slowly to his face as he became overly aware of her scrutiny.

"Did you get some rest last night or were you commanded to stand guard outside the door again?" she asked him.

He raised an eyebrow in mock surprise and looked at her. "You mean you did not bother to check on me in the middle of the night?" he asked in an exaggeratedly hurt voice.

It was now her turn to blush as she remembered the first night she had tried to sneak out of the room and Jason had caught her red handed. She threw a pillow at him with surprising accuracy, catching him in the face before it dropped to the floor. Picking it up, he tossed it back on the bed with an easy, indulgent smile. "I am well rested, thank you."

She was still wrapped in the covers and Jason could not help but wonder if she wore anything under them. Just to see her like that made him think that a man would need to have nerves of steel to keep from ravaging her repeatedly. He wondered how Logan had fared with the doctor's orders. He thought about how difficult it would have been for him if this woman belonged to him. He did not feel sure that he could have managed to stay away from her for an hour, let alone days.

"And you?" he asked, emphasizing his words meaningfully.

She looked back at him, smiling mischievously and stretching like a cat beneath the sheets. Jason had to exert tremendous will power to keep from dashing across the room and grabbing her up from the bed.

"Very well thank you," she said. "I thought that I might have landed you into hot water last night."

"Oh?"

"I blurted out to Logan one or two of the things we discussed yesterday," she continued, "but I can see that there are no secrets between you two."

Jason shook his head and looked squarely back at her with his sea green eyes. "None at all," he replied solemnly.

Was it just a statement or another warning? Kara had made mention of the matter to gauge his reaction and to ascertain how much she could trust him. She was pleased to know that Jason felt such loyalty towards Logan. She had no intentions of doing or saying anything that would place this man in a position that would require discretion.

"What's in the parcel?"

"A change of clothes."

Kara breathed an exaggerated sigh of relief as she grabbed the package and tore it open. "That's wonderful," she said brightly. "But I am beginning to feel like I will never have clothes in a closet again."

Jason said nothing to this. He was well aware that she had been clothing herself from parcels over the last couple of days but he also knew that soon enough this would change. "Have you been keeping to your end of the bargain?" he asked.

"Haven't you wheeled out the supper cart yourself?" she asked sweetly in reply knowing exactly what he was referring to.

"As much as I am pleased to see that it was almost empty, I cannot be sure that it was not the Captain who consumed most of it," he said with a lopsided smile.

"No you can't," she said "but you have also brought in a breakfast cart haven't you?"

"So I can witness for myself then?" he asked.

"Exactly," she said, throwing off the covers and walking with her torn package towards the bathroom. "Can you give me a few minutes of privacy?"

"Of course," he said, springing up, relieved and disappointed at the same time to see that she was almost fully dressed.

"Have you had breakfast yet?" she asked him.

"I have." he answered.

"Maybe you can still join me while I have mine. Is that ok?" she asked tentatively.

"Yes, of course. May I have a quick look around before you use the bathroom?"

Kara was already pushing aside the curtain to enter, but she stopped. Stepping back, she smiled. "Be my guest," she said, waiting patiently as he moved past her.

Once he had satisfied himself that nothing was left behind that could cause harm, he exited the bathroom and walked towards the door. "Thank you." she said quietly as he past her.

Jason stopped and turned around to face her.

"For what?" he asked, his brow knitted in puzzlement.

"For saving my life," she said humbly.

His face registered his surprise at her gratitude. "You are welcome," he acknowledged sincerely, his voice full of warmth.

"I will never knowingly put you in that position again." she continued softly.

"That would be greatly appreciated," he said with a smile. "I would not want to have to deal with the captain if something were to happen to you again."

Kara returned the smile in complete understanding before Jason left the room. She stood where she was leaning against the wall, enjoying her privacy for a moment. As much as she was comfortable with Jason in the room she was craving some time alone. Certain things were nagging at her and she wanted an opportunity to address them at leisure. As she brushed her teeth and showered she allowed her mind to finally address the errant thoughts.

Despite not having sex with Logan last night, she was indeed sleeping with the enemy — literally. Although Logan had not been unkind to her the fact still remained that both he and Jason had played significant roles in the downfall of her people and continued to be a part of their oppression. She wondered how she could have such a strong need for a man who could hurt people willingly on the one hand while professing his amorous feelings for someone of that same culture on the other.

By the time Kara returned to the room she continued to feel confused. She still had not sort through much that seemed duplicitous in Logan yet she felt sure that she would be able to make a difference in how Logan and Jason were influenced going forward.

Fixing a smile on her face, she threw open the door and Jason came back in. As they sat at the table Kara spoke to him about leaving later that day for her new living space. Once again Jason was open to sharing what information he could. "Logan is concerned that I will be in more danger there," she said.

"As will he; and by association me," said Jason soberly.

Kara looked at him perplexed. "Why?"

"When Logan first heard of what had happened to you, he came to the mediunit immediately. He was so agitated he almost gave himself away."

Kara had not known that Logan had even been there. Neither of the men had mentioned it before. She was not sure what Jason meant by his remark but she certainly felt gratified to know that Logan had come to see her after all.

"He already needed to make quite an effort to control and hide his obvious feeling for you."

"And having feelings for me a bad thing?"

Jason smiled indulgently. "If Logan is seen as crossing the line with you he could lose you or be punished for it. You are supposed to be viewed as property after all, not as someone who could claim a Giddian's heart."

Kara stared at Jason. His words held meaning on a number of levels. For one thing, it was yet another warning that he was passing along but for another, he seemed to imply that Logan had deeper feelings for her than was allowed.

"I have truly seen the error of my ways Jason, and I will try not to be difficult for you or him again," she said quietly, regarding him sincerely.

Jason could not help but smile. "That will help

to make my job to protect you a little easier,' he said, "and I really want to do my job well."

"Protect me?" she asked teasingly. "I thought you were preventing me from escaping."

"They can be one and the same thing," he retorted.

She knew exactly what he meant. There was now a shared understanding between them so they continued the conversation comfortably.

Chapter 19

Kara was required to make the trek to her new accommodations bound at the wrist. She was appalled, while Jason appeared tortured as he insisted. She wanted to argue with him but she had given him her word that she would not put up a fuss.

"I would not insist if I did not think it necessary." he said. "But we do not know who we are likely to meet along the way. Since I am the only one you will be with it will be viewed as too much of a risk to let you walk freely."

She acquiesced sullenly allowing him to place the restraint on her. The concession he made was to bind her hands in the front so she could be a little more comfortable. It was also safer for her in case she should stumble.

As instructed she kept her eyes to the ground and wore a blank expression on her face when they exited the elevator in the Brock Building and joined the throng of people bustling back and forth across the campus. They walked for about three blocks before Kara guessed their final destination. It was Riggs Hall that last night Logan had called Drumlin instead.

Riggs Hall was one of the more spacious and luxurious dorms that was often reserved for the children of the rich. There was even a fully fledged restaurant in the building rather than the dorm style cafeteria that was more typical of the other accommodations on campus.

There were no incidents along the way allowing Jason to breathe a sigh of relief as he entered the lobby of the building with Kara. He had told her that the apartment was on the very top floor. As they stood waiting for the elevator, the door slid open and Alfred stepped out.

"Sivirt!" he cried in surprise as Jason saluted him smartly. "I see that Logan has finally decided to join us. I am glad of it. Is there no one with you helping to bring his property here?"

"No one else was required," said Jason with confidence, "as you can see." He indicated the restraints on Kara's wrists.

"Yes, she does appear to be well in hand," Alfred said, giving Kara a contemplative look.

"I heard that she tried to take her own life," he continued. Kara felt a cold hand reach for her injured wrist. Her first impulse was to snatch her hand away from his vile touch and bolt for the door but she squelched the thought, forcing herself instead to keep her eyes focused on the ground. Even so, her heart hammered uncontrollably in her chest.

"It happened quickly and without warning," said Jason, "but it is not likely to occur again."

"Oh? And why is that?" asked Alfred with a gleam in his eyes as if he was relishing hearing the answer to his question.

"Because the captain has taken great pains to show his property the error of her ways," Jason said.

Grute laughed heartily at his remark. "I suppose I will have to get the details of how he managed to do that straight from the horse's mouth?"

"But of course sir," Jason said, with a cheeky, lopsided grin.

Alfred dropped her hand and placing his fingers under her chin, he tipped her head up to look at him. Kara did not resist even though she wanted to shut her eyes tightly against the scrutiny of the man.

"Look at me," he commanded.

She raised her eyes slowly to look into his. She was shocked at how cold they appeared. The blue of his eyes were so pale they could have been ice chips. He was smiling so coldly at her she thought she might collapse from fear. The emotion must have shown clearly on her face because he seemed to enjoy what he saw there.

"I can see that she has been broken in. I look forward to hearing how he managed to house train her." Alfred said. "Tell your captain I said he is lucky that she is not my type." He laughed loudly again and moved past them towards the door that led out of the building.

Jason had held the door to the elevator open while he conversed with Alfred. As they stepped into the small enclosed space, two more people joined them and travelled with them to the tenth floor. Kara remained standing silently next to him, her head still bent but he knew that she was only barely holding it together.

As they stepped out of the elevator, Kara saw that there were four doors leading off the corridor. Jason hustled her down the passageway to the one at the farthest end and wasted no time unlocking it.

She was beginning to tremble with pent up emotions, shocked by the encounter with the major and the manner in which they had communicated about her. Jason had found it difficult to seem so flippant about escorting a woman who was restrained and labeled the sexual property of another, but he'd had no choice. He needed to be convincing in the role he played no matter how much it hurt Kara.

As he ushered her in and closed the door behind him, she collapsed immediately to the floor and started to shake uncontrollably from the shock of her ordeal.

Jason felt powerless and unsure of what to do. At first he just stood there looking at her but then his instinct to protect and console her took over. He sank to the floor next to her and quickly removed her restraints. He pulled her into his arms and she did not resist, instead, Kara grabbed on to him desperately as he held her tightly.

"It's okay," he said, trying to sooth her. A part of him could not believe that he was actually holding her in his arms while she clung to him. If he had not been so concerned over her anguish, he would have indulged his senses and fully relish the moment. As it was, all he could manage was to close his eyes and inhale deeply of her wonderful scent. "You are safe now," he breathed into her hair. His voice was thick with his own emotion. "I am so sorry about the way I had to speak of you. But you did well." She could only nod as she grabbed on to him tightly and cried.

When Jason and Logan had spoken to her about what she could expect, it had seemed surreal. Kara had felt fairly removed from it all cocooned as she was in that basement room. But having made the trek across campus and surviving her encounter with Alfred, the truth of her situation was finally driven home in all its gravity.

That man had equated her to a house pet and had spoken about her being broken in. She finally understood that she was probably even worse off than a slave. She was convinced more than ever that she should stay put and follow the instructions of both Logan and Jason to the letter.

Jason held her saying nothing as he continued to

fight his own feelings of helplessness. He wanted to do so much more; find a way to take her away from all of this, even if it meant giving up his life to ensure her safety. But she did not belong to him and all he could do was trust that Logan would always be there for her.

At length Kara was able to compose herself sufficiently to get up off the floor. She dried her tears and looked around feeling fairly distracted by the inordinate amount of light coming into the large, spacious room.

After being in a tiny room without windows, it was a huge contrast. She was glad to see that there were large windows along one wall of the room. There was even a large skylight set high in the ceiling of the living room.

Jason watched her move around reveling in the space. He felt relieved that she had managed to pull herself into a better space so quickly. He could not begin to fathom how she must have felt to be so nonchalantly equated to a house pet.

They were in a room that held both a sofa set and a dining set. It was obvious that the dorm had been renovated because everything looked and smelled new. The bedroom was big, bright and airy while the bathroom included both a shower stall and a deep bathtub that could easily accommodate two. There was an abundance of towels as well as his and her toiletries. Kara could not help but feel much better inside.

There was only one other door in the bedroom that led into a walk-in closet. It was divided into his and her sections and was filled with clothes. There were clothes for Logan of course, but to her delight, there were lots for her as well, along with jewelry and shoes for every occasion.

Conspicuously, there was no kitchen in the apartment. As she was not sure how they were going to managed anonymity without a kitchen, she asked Jason about it.

"The captain will be required to take a number of his meals with the other officers in the restaurant on the ground floor of the building. But our meals will be delivered to us here." Kara was pleased that Jason was indicating that he would continue to stay with her.

She explored the rest of the suite and was glad to see a good selection of books and games on hand. She was hopeful that she could get Jason to play some of the games with her because it would be a welcomed way to pass the time in the apartment - at least at first.

Chapter 20

By the time Logan appeared at supper time, Kara had gotten over the trauma of her earlier encounter with Alfred and was in much better spirits. Logan saw the change in her and was pleased that she liked the apartment.

Their evening passed pleasantly enough each of them choosing to put aside the gloomy thoughts that tended to creep into their minds. Instead, they focused on enjoying each other's company.

Logan did not seek intimacy beyond holding her that night, or the next, but on the third night when he entered the room, the electricity crackled between them. Even Jason could not mistake their heighten state of anticipation and he took his leave as soon as he could, while Logan was only too happy to speed him on his way.

After closing the door behind Jason, he leaned against it and focused his attention on Kara. She was sitting on the couch with her legs folded beneath her, pretending to read a book. He looked at her with a hooded, predatory expression so that there was no mistaking the smolder in his eyes. The look was so elemental that Kara felt the need to spring up and meet him in full flight.

He covered the distance between them in just a few long strides. All she had managed to do was to get up from the couch before he was upon her. Casting off his jacket and pulling his shirt from his pants before he even reached her, he pulled her urgently into his embrace and possessed her mouth passionately.

Kara had made herself as ready for him as she dared with Jason there. She had taken great care with her toilet, anticipating his touch, and she had put on a simple, but pretty dress with thin shoulder straps. What she really wanted to wear was a black negligee that was so daring she had blushed on first seeing it, but she did not feel right to put it on while Jason was still in attendance.

Logan's tongue found purchase in her mouth, tangling almost instantly with her own. She was not even sure how he had managed to take off his trousers and underpants so quickly. In another instant he was hiking up her dress and laying her back on the couch even before he was quite finished with the kiss.

She had tried to tell him several times before that it was okay for him to be with her, but he had been stubborn. He had insisted that she use the time to recover, teasing her that she would need all of her strength when he finally decided to come to her. Now as he spread her legs and just pulled aside the crotch of her panties, she was not so sure he had been teasing.

The ferocity of his attack on her body made her instantly wet. She felt his gorgeous, mushroom headed cock pressing up against her for only a fleeting moment before he was driving his shaft swiftly home. Kara cried out in shock and intense pleasure at being taken so possessively. Only after he had imbedded himself fully inside her, did he still for a moment. Looking at her, he wanted to ensure that the suddenness of his attack had not caused her undue harm, but Kara's vagina was stretched and filled to the brim with Logan's cock. She was spread out before him on the couch like an offering and there was nothing left to do now but to bring their rite to completion.

"Take me," she whispered to him huskily. It was all the invitation he needed. His rhythm was strong and powerful from start to finish as he pumped himself into her vigorously. She was surprised at how quickly and violently she was cresting around his hard cock as she braced against his chest. Her nails were sinking into him as she cried out her pleasure loudly. She heard him grunt softly and felt the driving tempo increase even more. Within just a few more strokes, he was empting himself into her. His body was fused to hers; his cock completely buried in her tight, little cunt.

Kara was relieved that she had started on the course of contraceptives as soon as the doctor had given it to her. She felt that it was intercourse of such a nature that could instantly make her pregnant.

Logan shuddered violently with his own release. He kissed her mouth briefly before he sunk into her embrace. Shifting his position slightly, he slipped out of her and pulled her underwear back into place. He smiled and smoothed the hair out of her face where his determined drive piling into her body had rumpled the strands.

"I just could not wait to be inside of you," he said almost apologetically. Are you ok?" All Kara could do, was nod. He chuckled and asked her again. "Are you sure?"

"Yes," she said, panting. "As you can probably tell from my own reaction."

He kissed her happily. Getting off the couch, he lifted her into his arms and walked with her effortlessly into the bedroom. Laying her on the bed he quickly disappeared into the bathroom. Before long, Kara heard the water running as he returned to the room and undressed. She could only assume that he was running a bath and she was a little disappointed that he was planning to interrupt their love making. Already her body was craving him again. She did not want to wait for him to take a bath before she could have him again.

When he started to undress her, she recognized his intent and was only too happy to oblige him. They walked together into the bathroom where he directed her to enter the bath as the water rose. When he got into it with her, they continued to kiss and touch each other.

Kara soaped a washcloth and started to rub it leisurely along Logan's body. She enjoyed the look and feel of his muscles and skin glistening under the water. She straddled him, rising up on her knees to soap his neck.

His head was thrown back against the edge of the tub and his eyes were closed. She marveled again at the length and thickness of his lashes. They were wet with water and clumped together. Kara felt a stirring just at the sight of them. She dropped her eyes to focus on his lips. They were made for kissing she thought again just like she did on first seeing him. She kissed him and he returned it, grabbing for her to bring her closer, but she pushed away from him gently.

There was something that she had been dreaming of doing and this was her opportunity, so she did not wish to be distracted. His cock was already rising out of the water. She took a moment to turn off the tap as she did not wish for the tub to fill up any further.

She slid her naked body down his until she was breathing through her open mouth, right on the tip of his penis. Logan's eyes flew open and he tried to sit up. He gasped softly as she took him into her mouth and began sucking on him slowly.

Logan pressed against her gently for her to

disengage, but she resisted, and he did not insist. Instead, he watched her take his big cock into her mouth and he became fascinated with watching her tongue and suck him. All too soon he was bracing his head against the lip of the tub again, his eyes closed as she took him deeper into her mouth.

He raised his head and looked at her to make sure she was not gagging to accommodate him. He was encouraged by the expression of rapture on her face as she held his penis and focused on the task at hand. Without taking his eyes off her he began moving his hip in and out to match her sucking motion. The whole experience was so erotic that it was too easy for him to come in her mouth. He pushed on her urgently to break the contact because as much as he wanted to give up the struggle, he also wanted to bury himself inside her again.

As she sat up, he gently turned her away from him so that she was bracing against the edge of the tub. He got up on his knees and slipped into her from behind. As always, his smooth, firm entry as he lodged his cock inside her, was a delightful awakening. From the feel of him thrusting into her, she knew that he could feel her tightness gripping him.

Now that he was in control, he slowed down their love making and worked her over well, pumping his cock into her; first slowly, and then picking up the pace. Sometimes he would vary the angle slightly at which he entered her. His stamina was tremendous. He brought her to the edge several times before he would slacken his rhythm again, until she was frantic for her release. He finally took pity on her. When she came, she cried out her pleasure loudly, her body shuddering repeatedly with wave after wave of intense pleasure.

Logan had stilled inside her only long enough for her to fully enjoy her release before beginning his driving rhythm again. He stroked her insides from angles she had not yet felt. He grew even harder, swelling inside of her and stretching the walls of her vagina. The additional friction was just what she needed to begin cresting again and it was only then that Logan bent over and cupping her breasts from behind, he started pumping his cock into her until they were both shuddering violently, their cum mixing together inside her sweet cunt. Kara did not even know it was possible to come so many times. Logan himself was amused by the thought that his woman was most definitely multi-orgasmic and pleased to see her revel in what he could do to her body.

Eventually they came out of the bathtub and dried themselves off. Logan was far from finished with Kara, but he knew there was the need to interrupt their lovemaking for nourishment. He was aware that she might still be weak, and he did not want to push her too hard. What he really wanted was to love her as if there was no tomorrow which seemed apt in their current situation.

They ate supper quickly and quietly both sensing that tonight was not a night for conversation. When he felt sure that she'd had enough to eat, he took her to the bed.

"Now it is my turn," he said. "I have thought so often of tasting you again that I have been comparing everything I ate to you."

"And what have you concluded?" she asked, playfully.

"That, I can survive comfortably on a diet of you alone." His response took her breath away. When he trailed his hot mouth down her flat stomach to sink his tongue into her, she arched her body at his sudden invasion. She moaned loudly in absolute abandon as he troubled her clit mercilessly with his tongue. She felt a long thick finger slip inside her and she moaned again unexpectedly. She spread her legs even more, wanting to give herself totally over to the magic Logan was working.

Before he could completely unravel her, she pushed him away. "No!" she cried in a voice full of need. "Please take me now," she begged. "Please!" In a heartbeat, he filled her up and sent her spiraling, while her vaginal walls squeezed and slackened around his thick shaft in peristalsis motion. He continued to move in and out of her slowly, still controlling her body so that she clenched her stomach muscle more than a couple of times as he prolonged her ecstasy with his deliberate movement.

When Kara finally felt herself becoming aware of her surroundings again, she tried to recall how many times Logan had made her come already that night, but she was almost too delirious with exhaustion to care. Eventually when sleep claimed them both, she stayed in his arms well satiated and a little raw from having him inside her so much.

Chapter 21

Around noon on the following day, Jason was called away to run an errand, leaving Kara on her own. Even though he assured her that he would not be long, by four o'clock he had still not returned. Alone for far too long with her thoughts, she become depressed, thinking about her parents and what might have happened to them. She had thought about them often enough over the past few days but had not wanted to say anything about it to either Logan or Jason.

A key turned in the lock and the door opened abruptly, surprising her before she managed to compose herself fully. She was caught even more off guard when she saw that it was not Jason who entered.

"Logan!" she cried in confusion. "You are early."

"Yes I am Kara," he said, with a look of alarm on his face. "And I was not expecting to walk in to find you crying. What's the matter?" he asked with concern, as he came towards her.

Hardly able to contain her emotions, she rushed into his arms, crying unabashedly while he stood in the middle of the room and held her. He was completely at a loss for words.

Once she had quieted a little, he implored her to tell him what was wrong. She said that she had been missing her family and was longing for news of them.

Logan questioned her closely about them and found out that Kara was an only child with no close relations other than her parents. He wondered why she had never said anything about them to him before but he decided against bring it up. Instead, he reassured her that he would find out what he could, feeling sure that it should not prove too difficult.

With that promise, Kara became more composed. She asked how he had managed to return so early. "The officers have established a weekly dinner on Fridays for themselves and their property at the Rosemont restaurant downstairs. I am supposed to be there within the hour."

"Will I have to go?" she asked anxiously.

"While it might be expected, it is not compulsory. Unfortunately I do have to be there; at least for part of the evening." Logan shared no more information with Kara about the dinner but he seemed uneasy about having to attend the event.

When he was leaving for work earlier that day, he had heard Alfred swearing loudly at someone in his apartment. Things were crashing into the walls and a woman was crying hysterically. The commotion was loud enough for the officer who stayed in the apartment next to Alfred's to stick his head out into the corridor curiously. When he saw Logan, he just shrugged and laughed. "I guess it is just Grute going at his bitch again," he said, and closed his door in the most unconcerned manner.

Logan had stood for a moment, his heart pounding in his chest as he tried to grasp the reality of a situation that allowed for such things to be considered normal. Was he really a part of this new world? He wondered.

Later that evening, at the officer's dinner, he was shocked when Alfred arrived with the woman in tow. He was leading her by a chain attached to a collar around her neck. Despite the fact that she looked to be almost twice Alfred's height (Alfred was hardly above dwarf status) she appeared completely whipped. She sported a black eye and a busted lip, with a host of multi-coloured bruises everywhere that was exposed.

The other officers made light of the matter, teasing Grute about how quickly he managed to go through whores. Some of them were openly making bets as to how long they thought she would last. Most did not give her more than another week.

The gathering was exclusive to officers and their possessions as well as other high ranking officials. Many of them had shown up with their property and were engaging in a level of open promiscuity that was unbelievable. Men were having sex openly with their women as well as with those that belonged to other officers. Logan even had a fleeting glimpse of one woman in a darker corner of the restaurant being molested by at least two men simultaneously while a crowd gathered around them.

He felt the bile raise at the back of his throat as a sudden fear for Kara took hold of him and spread through his body like venom. He tried to get through his dinner quickly, and to keep it down while he forced himself to socialize with some of the other officers until he managed to gain the exit. Instead of taking the elevator to return to his apartment and Kara he felt the need for some fresh air and almost ran from the building to escape the scene.

Was this what he had signed up for? The ideal of his parents and what they had taught him to believe in was quickly becoming a far cry from the reality of the situation. He knew that the Mindaleans were considered property and he expected his people to lord over them, but was he purposely closing his eyes to the abject horror around him? Was he refusing to admit that what was happening was wrong? Was he afraid that having to admit to this would also mean that he too was guilty of committing atrocious crimes against the Mindaleans? Most importantly, would he have felt any different if he did not care for Kara?

Logan had turned a blind eye to the mass rape that had occurred when they had first invaded Mindalea. He had told himself that it was only to be expected. After all, such was the outcome of any war. But he had not set foot in the Kat House to see what was really happening to the women there.

Now he wondered how he was going to face Kara after what he had seen. How could he take her into his arms and pretend that the world that existed around them was as it should be?

Logan stayed out longer than he expected. When he finally returned to the apartment he was almost relieved to find Kara asleep. After dismissing Jason, he drew a chair up to the bed and sat looking at her in the dim light. He hoped that she would not stir or wake up. What could have happened to Kara if he had not chosen her to be with him? He shuddered to think about it, feeling only relief again in knowing that he had saved her from what he witnessed downstairs. There was a part of him that wanted to hold her tightly as if she was a lifeline to keep him from drowning, but there was another part of him that acknowledged the hypocritical nature of being with her.

He left her sleeping peacefully in the bedroom and retired to the living room. Hours later, he eventually fell into a fitful sleep on the couch. Saturday was his day off so there was no need for him to be up early.

Chapter 22

The ground shook as if from a tremendous blast. Logan sprang from the sofa as Kara came rushing into the room her eyes wide with fear. Before long, they were running from the building as fast as they could. There was mayhem everywhere as people ran helter skelter, screaming in fear. The sound of the emergency siren blared while Logan kept hold of Kara's hand and began running for his life. He was terrified - his only thought: save Kara.

He heard her cry out and felt her hand slip from his suddenly. He stopped abruptly and turned around. Already she was slipping down the side of a big sinkhole that had opened up in the ground. She was reaching for him and calling his name. He saw many hands reaching up from the hole, clawing at her and trying to drag her down. She screamed out his name frantically again and he tried to go back for her but found that he could not move.

Not wanting to tear his eyes away from her he watched helplessly as she slipped further away from him. A knot of fear inside him was suffocating him, while frustration and a deep sense of despair were threatening to overwhelm him. He became aware of something squeezing his chest and instinctively he knew that it was the reason he could not move. He looked down and saw a snake with a long, thick body winding its way around and up his torso, squeezing him tightly. When the snake's head came around to face him, Logan was looking right into the face of Alfred Grute.

"Logan!" he heard Kara scream again. His eyes sprang open. Kara was kneeling beside the sofa shaking him gently. She had been calling his name gently, trying

132

to wake him. He was drenched with sweat but when he saw her there, alive and whole, he grabbed her and held on tightly.

"You're alive," he whispered in relief. His heart felt full and happy. "Thank God you're alive."

"Yes I am alive, and I am safe. You were just having a nightmare."

"Yes a nightmare," he repeated, still shaken and preoccupied. He ran his hand through his hair, completely agitated and swallowed loudly; his mouth parched dry. Perceiving his need for water, Kara stood up to get some for him but Logan held on to her hand firmly. "Don't go," he begged. She immediately sat next to him and placed her arms around him, holding him close. He clung to her desperately completely relieved that none of it was real.

At length he was finally able to calm down, and he found himself wondering at the significance of seeing Alfred Grute in his nightmare. He could only assume that it was because he was so disturbed by Alfred's behavior towards his own property.

"Why are you on the sofa?" Kara asked, interrupting his sulky thoughts.

At first he said nothing because he was completely caught off guard by the question. "I came in very late last night and did not want to disturb you," was all he could manage lamely.

She smiled and kissed his forehead. "I am a woman at leisure, here for your pleasure," she said teasingly. "You can wake me at any time." She expected that her words would lighten his mood but instead she saw a dark shadow flit across his face.

"What is it Logan?" she asked, frowning. "You are completely out of sorts."

"It's nothing," he replied too quickly. "It will pass."

"Please tell me," she persisted quietly, and he could sense her need to know.

He sighed and pulled her even closer to him. "I was disturbed by my dinner with the officers last night," he said. "Suffice it to say, that I will never want to take you to one of those."

Kara did not press him for more information. She too was quite shaken by his reaction to his dream and felt that it was one can of worms she did not want to open. As she did not persist, he remained silent. Kara understood that her existence with Logan in their little world was not based on reality and that it could be taken away from her without a moment's notice. For now she was content to exist in her fantasy world for as long as she could manage.

She felt an overpowering urge to kiss him as if she could dispel the last remnants of his dream. She reached up and did just that. His response was so urgent that she was thrilled she could cause such a response in him. He held her not hungrily so much as desperately, and they proceeded to make love right on the carpeted floor of the apartment. Logan was more attentive and gentle than he had ever been with her before. There was a reverence to his lovemaking which made Kara feel completely treasured. It was almost as if he was trying to meld her body to his so that they could not be separated. When they were done, Logan made no move to take her to bed, or to even let her go so Kara stayed by his side and eventually fell asleep on the floor.

Sunlight was streaming through the skylight overhead when he awoke. It was not difficult to see why Kara preferred these living quarters to the little basement cell they had shared, yet being here was coming at a tremendous price.

He would have loved to take Kara for a stroll, or a picnic, but after what he had been exposed to the previous night, he was convinced that if he ever hoped to keep her safe, he could never let her out of the apartment. The thought was completely depressing because essentially she was his prisoner and there could be no doubt about it. He did not want that for her but he was not sure what he could do about it.

His dinner last night had put him in such a foul mood that he felt completely torn. One part of him wanted to continue to keep Kara near him while the other felt the need to be alone so that his dark mood would not bring them both down. It was one thing to leave early in the morning and return in the evening to partake in carnal pleasures with Kara, but seeing her caged up for hours on end plagued him with his powerlessness to change the situation.

It was not long before he told her he needed to return to the office. "But I thought this was your only day off," she said, completely disappointed.

The look on her face was enough to make Logan think twice about leaving her but he needed to get away even if it was for a short time. "It is. But it is also the only day I can investigate the whereabouts of your parents. There will be no one at the office." He was not lying but he hated what he had to do next. "I have given Jason the day off. Do you think you can manage without him today?"

Honestly, Kara did not think that she could. It would mean being locked away in the apartment alone for long hours and she had already had too much of that the previous day. At least when Jason was there she was able to keep the depressive thoughts at bay, but how would she cope by herself for hours on end?

"Of course," she answered bravely, but Logan hated himself even more when he saw that her reassurance had not reached her eyes. He simply nodded though and got up to take a shower. He convinced himself that it should not take long to find the information he would be seeking and that he would be back in the apartment sooner rather than later.

As they ate breakfast there was an uneasy silence between them. Logan continued to seem caught up in his own thoughts and Kara felt as if a distance was being created between them. It made a chill run through her. She felt sure that his change of mood had something to do with his dinner last night but she was too afraid of what he might reveal to ask him anything about it. When he left she felt like doing nothing so she crawled back into bed and pulled the covers over her head.

Chapter 23

As Logan headed towards the Brock building, he impulsively contacted Jason on his PI. "Are you at the barracks?"

"No sir." Jason replied, but offered no more information concerning his whereabouts. From his response, Logan gathered correctly that he was wrapped tightly in Gracie's arms and was not at liberty to say very much. Logan decided that under those circumstances he would not even broach the subject he had intended to.

"What do you need Captain?" Jason asked when there was only a pause at the other end.

"I have to go to the office for a few hours and I left Kara alone," Logan blurted out.

"Do you want me to report for duty?" asked Jason.

"I am not sure I should ask it of you Jason, this is after all your day off too."

"I can be there in an hour," Jason said.

"Maybe not Jason," Logan said. He thought to ask this of Jason now would mean that he would probably continue to impose on his time going forward. It was not fair to have him stay with Kara while he tried to escape the apartment. "I am not planning on being gone long, just disregard this conversation."

There was a brief silence on the PI. "Yes sir," Jason finally said and the conversation was over.

Logan experienced a moment of indecision. He wondered if he should just turn around and go back to Kara, but curiosity to find out about her parents had already taken hold of him and he had promised himself that he would just spend an hour or two and be back at the apartment before long.

Two hours stretched into three, and then four before he completely lost track of time. When he finally looked up from the research on his desk, he was still alone as he had been all day, but it was getting dark outside. He had left Kara alone for far too long.

Logan wrapped up what he was doing and headed back to the apartment at a brisk pace. Even so, there was time to think about what he had discovered, but more importantly what he had tried to discover and had not managed to.

When Logan had pulled up images of the drone footage on the town of Antworth where Kara's parents lived, he was shocked to see that the town no longer existed.

It had been flattened by Giddian bombs and there were no records of survivors from the blast. Logan was further disturbed when following a hunch, he found five other areas throughout Mindalea that had been bombed in a similar manner. By now he was horrified. Thousands of people had just been wiped clean from the world. Some of those towns and cities might have even contained Giddians who had not yet been processed and absorbed into the new Giddia.

As Logan continued his research, he saw a brilliant strategic pattern of destruction emerging. The bombings had occurred in areas where it was determined that the Giddians' diminished forces would be able to strike and conquer Mindalea almost instantly. Mindaleans outnumbered Giddians on a ratio of about ten to one, yet many large areas of Mindalea were already under Giddian control. He had thought that the invasion had occurred quickly because the Mindaleans had just given up easily. Now he was not so sure.

Logan's research took him into areas of classified information that was blocked even to his code. He spent a lot of time trying to break through the protective walls discreetly to see what he could find. General Degan was a huge proponent of ensuring that the Giddians operated as individual pods and had been diligent to ensure that one pod was not very aware of what another was doing.

There were two fairly large projects that Logan found to be of particular interest. Despite the fact that one appeared dated there was another that looked like it had only recently been started. It was clear that based on the reoccurring file names they were connected in some way. There was also the name of a place *Trio*s that kept popping up. Beyond that Logan found it almost impossible to access any more information.

He was not familiar with Trios as the name of a place that currently existed in Mindalea so he assumed that it was probably a Giddian facility that was only recently set up. He was tempted to stay and try to figure out what he could about the place but any additional searching would have to wait until the following Saturday.

On any given day he could not wait to return to the apartment to see Kara. Today however his heart grew heavier the closer he got to Drumlin Hall. What was he going to tell her about her parents? He felt weighted down inside and dreaded facing her.

When he arrived at the apartment he was surprised to see Jason there. He and Kara were sitting comfortably in the living room playing a game of Yunkle.

"Jason! What are you doing here?" Logan asked as he removed his jacket and hung it on a peg by the door.

"Didn't you get my message?" Jason countered puzzled. "I have been here since ten o'clock this morning."

Logan knitted his brow as he pulled out his PI. He had not paid any attention to it because there was no reason for anyone to be trying to reach him today. When he saw the message from Jason saying that he would report for duty immediately, he looked sheepish. "I somehow must have missed that. I had no idea you were here otherwise I would have tried to make it back earlier."

Kara pouted as she sashayed up to him. She stood on tiptoes and placed a brief kiss on his lips in front of Jason. They had all become very comfortable with each other and no one seemed to mind. "You mean it would have been okay for you to leave me alone here for your entire day off with just crackers and water?"

Logan felt deeply embarrassed. He had not even thought that she would be locked away with no means of getting a meal. As much as he felt horrible all he could think to do was try and change the subject. "I am truly sorry that I was away so long but as I recall, I was on a mission to gather intelligence for you." At his admission, Kara's eyes lit up with hope and Logan instantly regretted trying to change the subject.

"Have you found out something about my parents? Where are they now? Are they safe?" Kara asked eagerly. It was clear from her words that she had already shared what he had been up to with Jason but Logan did not mind. He trusted Jason to keep their secrets.

"I have not been able to find any records

concerning them yet," he lied. When he saw her face fall instantly, it was like a blow to his heart for his deceit. "But I will try again next Saturday," he said quickly. "I will not be able to do anything until then."

Logan glanced over her head and saw that Jason was observing him closely. His throat constricted because he knew that Jason must have seen right through his response. He would know that there was no way that he could not have found out something about her family by now.

Antworth was well within the new borders of Giddia and already detailed reports were in place about most of the Mindaleans in captivity. Jason remained silent though. After a quick debrief and Logan's sincere thanks for being there, he left with the promise to return the next day at his regularly appointed time.

While it was clear that Kara was disappointed, she was also buoyed up by the fact that he was planning to try again for the information the following Saturday.

As they had supper, he was fairly quiet. Kara felt like she needed to make up for it by giving him details about how she had spent her day and some of the things that Jason had said was happening around her.

Logan was more than content to sit and listen to her but when the meal was over, he took her to bed without delay. That night, their love making was extremely tender. Logan spent a lot of time touching and tasting her. To Kara it almost felt like he was worshiping her body and it was intensely erotic.

They continued to say little to each other but Kara was fairly convinced that something continued to rest heavily on Logan's mind. She tried to ask him about it but all he said was that while he was looking for leads on her parents he had come across some unrelated information that he wanted to investigate further.

As Kara continued to be mindful of not wanting to spoil their time together she did not press him further. She too was aware that every moment they spent with each other was precious and so she gave herself over to making as many wonderful memories as she could with him.

Chapter 24

The week that followed fell into a pattern. Logan left early in the morning while Jason joined Kara for the day. When Logan got back around supper time Jason would leave for the night.

Kara's relationship with Jason grew stronger every day and if he had feelings beyond friendship for her he kept them well in hand which helped to put her at ease.

She liked Jason a lot but her thoughts were always occupied with Logan. Her days were more or less spent in anticipation of his arrival for supper and the nights they would spend together.

It was disconcerting to see that Logan appeared more drawn every evening as if he was shouldering some burden that grew heavier each day. He refused to share anything about his troubles with her, but he continued to keep her very close while he was in the apartment.

His mindset was now very different from before the invasion. For one thing, he realized that on the whole, Giddian men saw themselves as superior to their own women so their behavior towards Mindalean women was even more reprehensible. He was also beginning to question why they had really invaded Mindalea at all.

On Wednesday morning when he was leaving the apartment, two mediunit attendants were wheeling a covered personnel cart out of Grute's apartment. As Alfred was not in attendance Logan became alarmed.

Before he could ask the attendants anything he saw that the covered form was too tall and too slender to be Alfred. His blood instantly ran cold. As he waited with the attendants for the elevator to arrive he had a horrible suspicion and felt an overwhelming urge to lift the sheet and peer under it. There was a part of him that was fearful of what he might see so he initially resisted the urge.

Suddenly realizing that his position naturally granted him the right to know what was going on, he casually lifted the sheet and peered into the pale, dead face of Alfred's property. Although he knew that he should not have been so surprised he was actually stricken to see the young, inert form lying beneath the white sheet.

Immediately the memory of the officers making bets at the dinner about how long they expected the girl to last came flooding back to him. Somehow he did not think that they meant how long she would stay alive but rather, how long they thought she would continue to be with Alfred before he grew tired of her and did something that was likely to land her in the mediunit.

"I guess she didn't last very long," he forced himself to say nonchalantly, hoping to start a conversation that would get him more information.

The two male attendants snickered. "No surprise," one of the attendants answered, leaving Logan to surmise what he would from his remark.

The elevator arrived quickly and Logan directed the men to proceed before him. "What was the eventual cause of death?" he asked, as the two men wheeled the gurney into the small elevator.

"Multiple shots," said one of them. Logan felt shock run through him.

Right up the cunt," said the other, "She must be fried inside." The two men snickered again while bile rose up the back of Logan's throat. He must have turned green, he thought.

"You coming sir?" asked one of the men as he held the elevator door to prevent it from closing.

Logan shook his head. "You go on ahead. I just remembered something I left behind," he mumbled, almost inaudibly.

He moved quickly back down the hall as the elevator door closed. With shaking hands he fumbled to insert the key into the lock and opened the door to his suite. Before he had quite managed it Jason threw open the door quizzically, but Logan only pushed past him wordlessly and rushed into the bathroom.

He barely had time to close the door before he was retching loudly into the commode. His stomach was empty because he usually just settled for a cup of tea at his desk in the mornings, but this did not prevent him from dry heaving until he felt like he could hardly take in a breath. Kara's concerned voice could be heard at the door, asking if he was okay. She wanted to know if he needed her.

"I will be right out, I just need a moment," was all that he could get out at some point. He stayed in the bathroom for long minutes trying to compose himself once he had finished cleaning up. He knew he could not stay in there much longer without rousing their suspicion so eventually he exited the bathroom with his professional face painted back on.

"Are you ok?" Kara asked coming towards him, her face full of concern.

"I am now," he said. "I must be coming down with something." Logan hugged Kara to him, tightly but he could not look her in the eyes and he did not kiss her.

As he headed back towards the door with no

more explanation than that she called to him. "Don't you think you should stay here today and rest?"

He smiled regretfully at her. "I wish I could," he said, before leaving. He had no doubts that they would be perplexed by his behavior but he was not up to facing either of them at the moment.

Chapter 25

By the time Friday rolled around again, Logan was in complete turmoil. Now that he was observing more closely he saw numerous incidences of mistreatment and even cruelty towards the Mindaleans - especially the women.

He had lived among them all his life without taking the time to really get to know them. Between his parents and the school for Giddian boys he attended, he had lived in a bubble of Giddian ideology and aspirations, becoming effectively brainwashed into seeing Mindalea through the myopic lens of his people. His involvement with Kara forced him to see clearly how his actions had contributed to the downfall of her people.

His shame was almost too much to bear. By the evening when he was preparing to make an appearance at the Rosemont restaurant, he was beginning to feel more Mindalean than Giddian. Logan was now living constantly in fear - not for himself, but for the one he protected. Everywhere he went, he saw people who he felt would try to take Kara away from him.

Logan was appalled to see Alfred parading yet another tall, blond beauty in chains at the dinner. At one point in the night when Alfred approached him, he had to fight his urge to walk away before the squat, little man could get to him.

"Here alone again Logan?" he asked, as he led the poor woman on her leash.

"Of course," said Logan as if this was the only logical option for him.

"Yes, I forget that you are a very private person and would not dream of bringing your bitch here,"

Alfred said a bit testily.

Logan was enraged to hear him refer to Kara so. He felt like reaching across and punching the man hard enough to break his jaw. How had he tolerated this awful streak in Alfred before? Maybe it was not as apparent before the invasion as it was now. Either way, he fought to hold himself in check and ignore the comment.

"As I recall, you really wanted your little treasure," Alfred said with a smirk. "Is she proving to be all that you imagined?"

"I'm enjoying her," Logan said simply. There was something about Alfred's remark that made a red flag go up for him, but he was not sure why.

"Good. You will have to bring her down sooner or later, you know. You can't keep her hidden away from the rest of us forever."

Logan felt his throat tighten. This time he wanted to close his hands around Alfred's fat neck and just squeeze until the man's eyes bulged.

"Let me have a few more weeks with her before I consider sharing her," he said instead.

"I guess that is only fair. What do you think about my latest acquisition?" Alfred asked, changing the subject as he played with the chain attached to the collar around the girl's neck.

"Is she new? I didn't notice. What happened to the other one?"

"She lacked spirit," Alfred replied dryly.

Logan felt his jaw wanting to tighten again and he worked hard at remaining calm. "How did you come by your present boon?" he asked, curiously glancing at the tall, blond woman briefly.

She was dressed from neck to ankle in tight

fitting purple leather with a glossy sheen. Had it not been for the oppressed look on her face, Logan could easily see her as some female warrior in a sci-fi novel. There were zippers on her outfit that would allow easy access to her breasts and crouch, and was definitely an outfit that was meant to be worn in the privacy of a bedroom rather than in a public setting. But Logan had already determined that thoughts of propriety were not a dominant trait in the officers around him.

"She is from the Kat House, but I picked her up at the hospital. Apparently she had to be treated for some minor issue. Since Doctor Quiste knew that I needed a replacement, he thought I should check her out before he ended up sending her back. I could hardly refuse such an invitation - especially since he seems to know my taste so well."

Logan felt a cold hand grip his heart. Would Kara have suffered a similar fate at the hands of the good doctor if she had spoken out against him in the mediunit? He felt like rushing up to his apartment and taking her into his arms and never letting her go. Instead he made himself reach out and pat Alfred on the back as he had often done when they worked more closely together before the invasion. "Good for you Alfred," he said. "Hopefully you will make this one last considerably longer. I think the general was right. There may not be many more Mindalean women who are as tall as you like them."

"A pity," Grute acquiesced, regretfully.

Logan was relieved when another officer joined them just then, allowing for the conversation to shift to other topics. He wanted to leave early again like he had done the previous Friday but there was something in Alfred's manner that warned him against it. He had come under the man's direct scrutiny and he was determined to stay and play it off as unconcernedly as he could.

When it was finally time to make it up to his apartment, he found himself in the same frame of mind as before. He was experiencing such self loathing that he did not dare to lay with Kara. How could he have been so blind? His people were monsters. They operated as a unit without a conscience, and yet he as an individual felt ashamed and guilt-ridden on many counts.

Kara found him sleeping on the couch the next morning but thought little of it. She only reiterated that he could join her even if he came in while she was asleep. "In fact I welcome it Logan." she insisted.

He kissed her gently on the nose. "I will definitely try and remember that the next time," he said. "The couch is not nearly as warm and as soft as you are."

Shortly after breakfast, he left again for the office to continue his research. Jason had suggested he spend the Saturdays with Kara until Logan was able to be there with her. He had accepted his offer with a measure of relief but he also felt guilty about leaning on Jason so much - especially since he had yet to mention to him what he had really been up to.

Despite Jason's loyalty, Logan did not want him any more tangled up in his affairs than he needed to be but knowing that he would eventually need to share some of the information with him, Logan told Jason about the incident that had brought him back to the apartment to throw up. He was as shocked as Logan had felt and did not need to be told that he should stay even more on top of his duties to protect Kara.

Chapter 26

He arrived the next morning just as Logan was getting ready to head out the door. Like the previous Saturday, he was dressed casually. Today he wore a long sleeved, white shirt tucked neatly into a pair of fitted trousers, along with running shoes. It was still considered his day off after all.

Kara thought that as cute as he looked in his military uniform, she preferred seeing him like this. He seemed even more young and innocent but she was very aware that Jason was no boy. There was something about him that indicated that he could be as dangerous as Logan. Maybe it was even more lethal because it was so convincingly hidden behind an unassuming visage.

She had been almost hopping from one foot to the other trying to contain her excitement. She felt that today was going to be a big day for her. For one thing, she was sure to have some news of her parents when Logan got back. Kara had also determined that she was going to get a little more personal with Jason than she had managed to before. She had thought from the start that Jason's loyalty to Logan went well beyond the call of duty so today she was planning on finding out why.

She made a big show of ensuring that she ate her lunch well so that he would notice. When they sat down a little later to play a game of Yunkle she let him set up the game.

"Did you know Logan before the two of you joined the military?"

Jason's hand stopped suddenly in the midst of setting up the pieces on the board. He glanced up at her, piercing her with his lovely eyes to let her know that he was not fooled by her nonchalant question.

Kara tried to ignore the look but when he said nothing and resumed putting the pieces on the board, she persisted. "Please Jason," she pleaded, "I really would like to know."

Jason stopped what he was doing entirely and rocked back on the chair across from her. He regarded her closely as she forced herself to maintain candid eye contact with him. He looked powerful and imposing even though he sat in such a relaxed manner.

She could see that he was struggling with something internally and felt like she understood his hesitation. Jason was naturally exposed to all parts of her life, including the parts that were private to her and Logan. He was there after all to protect and serve them both and he needed to be in the know to do that competently. But in order to maintain his professionalism his own privacy and anonymity were important.

"He ensured that I had this opportunity in the military, and for that I will be eternally grateful," he finally said quietly hoping that such an explanation would be enough for her but he should have known better.

Kara was surprised by his response. Logan did not seem that much older than Jason so now she was even more intrigued about how one ended up serving the other. She continued to look at him expectantly without saying a word.

He sighed in exasperation as he usually did when she was especially persistent. Jason had already noticed that Logan had the same reaction to her but it was difficult for either of them to refuse her anything.

"I was just eleven years old," he began slowly, and very hesitantly. "My parents had just died and I was taken to a school for Giddian boys here in Brevika. The boys at the school ranged in ages from eight to sixteen and were being trained so that they could serve Giddia usefully in some capacity. Many of them still had at least one or both of their parents but there were some of us who had no close living relations."

"Logan had already been there at least two years before me. He too had lost both his parents so during breaks at school, when the other kids could return home to their families, a small group of us stayed on at the school all year round."

Jason paused. There was a part of him that wished he could stop there but there was another part that found it liberating to talk to Kara about it. She continued to look at him expectantly.

When it was apparent that he was not going to be let off the hook, he plunged on. "I was despised by the other kids when I first arrived." He glanced at Kara and saw the questioning look in her eyes, but he was not ready to go into that part of the story yet. "Let's just say that most of them believed that my parents were less than patriotic to the Giddian cause."

Kara remained silent, respecting his decision to tell only what he wished.

"Logan was the only one who did not give in to the peer pressure to ostracize me. Instead, he befriended me and stood up for me at every turn. I was puny at the time and considered a weakling, so he often found me being beaten up by one boy or another and had to pull them off me."

"He was easy going and very popular. At age fourteen he was the only boy who was leaving the school on a daily basis to work on a project that his parents had spear headed before they died."

"He was also a favorite with the general which was not to be taken lightly. Everyone knew, and respected him for it. When it became clear that Logan had taken me completely under his wing, I was still never liked but eventually I was tolerated."

"I could work well in the sciences so I was going to be recruited to work in the medical section but all I really wanted to do was to become a soldier and serve under Logan."

"The drill instructor did not even want to take a second look at me because I was so small, but Logan, even as a boy, stepped in somehow on my behalf. The adults around him were already accustomed to listening to him. They treated him as though he was part of their command structure, so Logan got his wish."

"I put my head down and trained to become the best soldier that I could possibly be so that I would not let him down. Hopefully I did not turn out too badly," he said, looking at her and grinning mischievously.

Jason was well aware that he could no longer be considered weak or puny. If anything, his fitness and physique could probably rival Logan's chiseled body. Of course she had never seen Jason without his clothes to prove that theory. Kara could not help the blush that spread slowly up her neck concerning her errant thoughts.

"I am sorry if I have made you uncomfortable," Jason said to her, but it was clear from the smug tone of his voice and the twinkle in his eyes that he was not the least bit sorry. If anything he appeared quite pleased with her discomfort.

She threw a cushion at him for teasing her and it dispelled the mood completely. There were many other questions Kara would have liked to ask him but the moment had passed and she was still embarrassed that he had caught her wondering what he looked like under his crisp, white shirt. Letting them both off the hook, she immediately turned her attention to the gaming board.

Logan was alone in the office once again. By mid-day he had finally managed to determine at least where Trios was located. Since he was not able to glean much more after hours of research, he decided that he would need to make a trip out there himself. It was too far to travel to that day so he used his technical expertise to secure an airborne drone with recording lens capabilities. He reprogrammed it for a new assignment and maneuvered it to the site where Trios was likely to be.

It was not hard to find the large facility sitting in the middle of nowhere. As far as Logan could tell it appeared as an abandoned building. He brought the drone in as close as he dared without drawing undue attention. There was movement that he was able to identify close to the site. When he honed in on the spot, he saw two, covered cargo mobiles moving slowly towards the gates of the facility.

There was no guard booth on the fenced perimeter of the grounds surrounding the building. The mobiles came to a stop at the gate while one person alighted from a vehicle to open it. The mobiles drove through and continued on toward the building.

Once the vehicles stopped, Logan saw people being off loaded from the back their hands bound behind them. They were corralled in the yard of the building by the Giddian soldiers who had come with the mobiles. The group stood waiting, but no one entered the building. Instead, a number of people in white medicoats eventually came out and escorted the group of prisoners in. The soldiers then returned to their vehicles and drove out of the compound, closing the gate behind them.

Logan had kept the drone overhead for as long as he dared. He was just about to leave the site when he saw a similarly covered cargo mobile leave the back of the building. On a hunch, he moved the drone to follow the vehicle hoping that it would not be on a long journey. He needn't have worried. The mobile stopped just a few miles from the facility at a large open area where the dirt looked like it had been freshly turned.

He watched in horror as uniformed men hoist inert bodies from the back of the vehicle and threw them down a steep incline. There were at least five that were taken from the mobile before an excavating machine began working to cover over the bodies with massive amounts of dirt.

Logan pulled the drone out of the area and sat for long minutes staring at his Data Analyzer. Alarm bells were going off in his head, but he had so little information about what he saw that he felt he could continue to stay in denial about what was happening - at least until he managed to make the trip to Trios.

He would now have to wait another week before he could check out the facility next Saturday but he was anxious about needing to wait that long. Inside he felt like he was running out of time. A hangman's noose was beginning to tighten around his neck, but he was not sure why.

As he dragged his feet back to the apartment he was struggling with what he would tell Kara. She would be expecting to hear something concerning her parents this time and he dared not put her off again. It was important to him that she continued to trust him so he felt that the only course of action open to him was to tell her the truth.

Chapter 27

As he entered the apartment, Jason stood from the couch immediately to attention, but Logan waved for him to be at ease. He told the captain that he had ordered Kara to bed a couple of hours before because she was growing too agitated waiting for him.

Logan nodded sadly. "She is expecting news of her parents today."

"And will there be any for her?"

"Yes," Logan sighed. "Unfortunately it is going to have to be the truth." He quickly filled Jason in on what he had discovered, or rather not discovered about Kara's parents.

Jason was shocked. "What the hell is going on?" he exclaimed when Logan told him about the other towns that had also been leveled to the ground, but he could only shake his head worriedly in response.

When Jason left, Logan took a deep breath bracing himself to enter the bedroom. Kara was fast asleep and he relieved that he had managed to put off having to tell her about her parents - at least for a little longer.

He watched her sleeping peacefully for a few minutes then went back into the living room. He poured himself an extra large drink and sat down on the sofa to brood. A short while later he heard movement in the bedroom before Kara appeared, slight and beautiful.

"Logan you are back," she said, with such a winning smile that he felt wretched inside. She knelt before him to hug and kiss him and he put aside his drink to take her up into his lap. "I did not hear you come in. Have you been back long?"

"No," he said with a smile Kara could not help thinking seemed sad. "It's only been about a half an hour now."

"Why didn't you wake me?" she asked. "You know I have been anxious to hear what you have found out about my parents." Before he could respond, she continued. "Have you found out something? Are they safe? Where are they?"

She was hugging him so he wrapped his arms around her and looked deeply into her eyes. There was a moment when she saw the pain flash in his eyes and her own face began to change. "What has happened Logan? Please tell me," she begged in a tremulous voice.

"I am so very sorry Kara." He paused, unable to get past the lump in his throat. He was devastated at the look on her face, and he could already see that she was slipping away from him. "I believe your parents are dead," he said sadly in resignation. He watched the color drain from her face and immediately wondered if there was not some easier way to break the news to her.

"No Logan. You could be mistaken," she said in a soft whisper. "How do you know they are gone? Just last week you said that you could not even find them. Maybe your records are wrong," she said speaking quickly now, desperately trying to find hope in something that he could say to her. "Maybe they're alive somewhere that you just don't even know about."

The tears had started to come, and there was nothing he could say to give her hope. He tried to hold her but she pushed away from him and sprang to her feet. He stood up too. "Are my parents really dead?" she asked incredulously.

"It was a bomb Kara," he said quietly. "It took out the whole town." Logan had never felt so low in his

159

life.

She blinked as if trying to comprehend what he had just said to her. "The whole town of Antworth is gone?" Logan was not able to respond audibly. All he could do was look at her, silently pleading for forgiveness as if he had personally dropped the bomb himself.

When Kara realized that he was saying nothing that would allow her hope she felt completely broken inside. "This can't be true. You bastard, you're lying!" she screamed, as she flew at him. "What kind of monsters are you?"

She was pounding on his chest with all her might yet Logan hardly felt the blows. He tried to hold, and steady her, but she pushed away from him. "Get away from me!" she yelled in a rage. "I hate you! Look at what you have done. You are no different from any of the others outside that door. I was a fool to think that you were." Her words cut him to the quick.

She ran from the room and he tried to go after her, but she screamed at him. "Stay away from me!" She slammed the bedroom door shut and collapsed on the bed, crying hysterically.

Every fiber of his being wanted to go to her but how could he? Everything she had said was true. He had been a fool to believe in a cause that he could hardly justify now. If anything he was far worse than many of the people around them. After all, it was through his efforts with the Dunlop Dampener that much of the death and destruction had occurred.

Logan sat down on the sofa with his head in his hands. For the first time since the death of his own parents, he wept. His despair was so overpowering he felt as if there was nothing he could ever do to make any of this better. Eventually as his self-pity began to recede it was replaced with a firm resolution to do something about the situation.

There was no supper cart that night because he did not even bother to order any. He had no appetite for food and he knew that Kara would not eat either. He opened the bedroom door once to check on her but went no further in. Kara cried for hours and his heart broke seeing her so wretched. It was truly one of the worst nights he had ever experienced.

At some point he must have dozed off on the sofa because he was suddenly awoken by a soft, rustling sound. When he opened his eyes he saw her moving quickly towards the front door. Logan sprang from the coach and got there just as she was opening it. He slammed the door shut and stood against it to face her. "What are you doing?" he cried in alarm.

"I am getting out of here Logan," she said, looking at him with determination.

"And where are you planning on going?" he asked. "Do you think that you can even make it out of this building without being caught?"

"So let them catch me," she shouted, livid with rage. "Why should I delay a fate that is meant for me anyway? Better I should die with my eyes wide open than to be locked away in here with you."

Her words stung him. "You do not mean that," he said trying to sound reasonable. "You are distraught. Please come back to the sofa." She pushed against him and struggled to get beyond him, but he held on even more desperately. "Kara, I cannot let you go!"

She sagged against him suddenly as if all the fight had gone out of her. Bending her knees, she sank slowly to the floor, taking him with her. "You have helped to slaughter my people Logan, and as much as I have tried to live this lie, I can't anymore," she said brokenly. Logan could find no words to reply. "I think that I am falling in love with you. Yet how can I? You will always be a part of something that has brought so much hurt and destruction to my life."

To hear her profess her feelings for him took his breath away. He too knew beyond a doubt in that moment that he had already fallen in love with her - enough to die for her. He took her into his arms and she did not resist.

"Kara look at me," he said, his voice filled with pain. She shook her head and refused, as the tears began to stream down her beautiful face. "Kara, please," he pleaded. It was the anguish in his voice that finally made her look up at him. She was surprised to see that his eyes shone with unshed tears.

"I swear on my life that I will get you to safety."

Even in her own grief she could not bear the thought that he was suffering. She could not help herself. She put up a trembling hand to touch his cheek as she smiled sadly through her tears. "To what avail, Logan? Where will I be safe? Your people are slaughtering mine with bombs that can wipe out entire towns and we do not have the means to fight back. Soon there will be none left to oppose your general."

Logan felt flabbergasted at her words. She was right. Even if he could get her out of Straveng, where would he take her? And even if he managed to get her to her own people, it was only a matter of time before they would all be wiped out.

He gathered her slowly into his arms and she let him. He held her silently as she cried herself into exhaustion on the floor. When he finally got up he lifted her into his arms and carried her to the bed. She didn't protest but lay quiet and still, even when he slipped into bed and continued to hold her.

Chapter 28

When he was ready to leave the next morning, Kara still had not shifted from her position on the bed. Logan was saddened by this but he was determined to push forward with his day. He now had the beginnings of a plan that could truly save her and there was a lot he needed to do in order to make it work.

On seeing Jason he could only report that she was devastated by the news. He was hopeful that Jason would have better luck rousing her from her depressive state, but even though he checked in more frequently during the day, it was no use. Each time Jason could only report that she had not even gotten out of bed. He sounded as disappointed as Logan felt. When he tried to get her to eat something she threw a book at him and yelled for him to leave the room.

Jason looked at him dejectedly when Logan walked in at the end of the day. He just shook his head in exasperation before he left the apartment. There was nothing to debrief the captain on that day.

Kara was awake but still had her back turned to him. Logan ordered supper then walking by her without a word he entered the bathroom and set the water to run in the tub.

Coming back into the room he scooped her up from the bed like a limp, rag doll. She did not protest but she looked at him listlessly as he walked with her slowly into the bathroom. Her face was tear-stained, and she appeared exhausted even though she had not gotten out of bed at all.

He set her down and gently began undressing her. She let him do it, cooperating enough so that it was not difficult for him to get her clothes off. When he was finished, she allowed him to pick her up and deposit her into the tub. He did not try to get in with her but sat on the floor instead almost fully clothed except for his jacket. He began to gently wash her body.

At first she did not respond to his touch. Before long though, she sighed almost as if in resignation. Turning to face him she pulled him gently to her and kissed him tenderly. It was an offering of reconciliation and he took it like a drowning man reaching for salvation. As he kissed her back, relief and wonder were apparent in every caress of his lips and every stroke of his tongue but he still made no move to join her.

"Please come in with me," she pleaded quietly. He looked at her searchingly to make sure that this was really what she wanted. As he kissed her again more urgently she responded as if to give him permission to do more. He stood up and undressed quickly before joining her in the hot water.

"I know that I am possibly in very grave danger," she said, "but I only just realized that I would rather be here with you for whatever time we have together than anywhere else without you," She lifted her left hand and looked at the thin white line across the wrist that was the only reminder of her recent folly. They had both marveled at how quickly the wound had healed. With a slight cringe Logan remembered remarking with pride how superior Giddia's technology was when compared to what he had seen in Mindalea.

"I told you that I will never attempt to take my life again," she continued gravely, "and I will hold to that promise. Now I am telling you that you do not have to worry, I will not try to leave this apartment again, unless it is with your permission."

His heart felt like it was overflowing with

gratitude. He reached across and kissed her again, only this time it was her turn to cling to him. They sat in silence in the tub both relieved that they had made up.

"There is a rumor that a large group of your people is finally being protected by your military," Logan said, after a while. "It appears that despite their handicaps, they are managing to find ways to fight back," He was holding Kara closely as he spoke. "I am going to get you out of here," he said with quiet determination. "I promise. I just need a couple of weeks to come up with a plan so that I can do it safely."

What he said should have thrilled her, instead it only made her anxious. She held on to him even tighter. "I don't know if I can go anywhere if it means being without you," she responded. They both knew that it was a long shot for him to follow her into Mindalean territory. He was likely to be shot on sight.

She looked up at him and he kissed her again, his heart filled with relief for her unconditional love. The kiss effectively brushed aside all thoughts of escape and death as they both became simultaneously aware of their urgent need for each other.

Kara thrust her tongue boldly into his mouth. It was an invitation to which he responded with all his ardor and passion. He pulled her on top of him and she was more than ready to slip down his rock, hard shaft until he was completely submerged inside of her. Logan kneaded her breast gently and she threw her head back. He looked at the column of her throat and reached up to kiss and suck gently on the smooth skin of her neck. Kara suddenly groaned and left off any attempt to make love to him in a leisurely fashion.

She began to fuck him roughly, tearing at his mouth with her own. Her movements on his penis were quick and almost savage as she rammed herself down onto him again and again. She became completely self-centered and lustful, tightening her vagina around him as she continued to worry his shaft in a rough frenzy. He was on the brink of pleasure in no time. She became strangely triumphant when she felt him become even harder inside of her.

He came with a roar, holding on to her desperately, trying to fuse her pussy to his body as he exploded inside of her but she would have none of it. She ground herself mercilessly onto him until she came in a burst of stars. Kara watched Logan keep his eyes tightly shut as he shuddered uncontrollably inside her.

The bath had suddenly become too hot as heat rolled off both of them. Water had also sloshed to the ground everywhere. Logan was in awe of what Kara had just done while she felt smug about her new found power over him. This was the first time that she had truly controlled their love making and kept Logan at her mercy.

After they got out of the bath, they ate quickly, satisfied that they were no longer at odds with each other but unable to ignore the fact that they were not entitled to be happy while the rest of the world fell apart around them.

When supper was over they continued their love making in a tempestuous manner. Logan was only too aware that Kara was bent on punishing him that night. She teased him mercilessly with her body until all he could think about was burying his cock repeatedly in her and finding release. She was clearly in control and he had suddenly become her plaything. He was completely turned on by his little dominatrix and more than happy to play his part.

Chapter 29

The relationship among the three of them relaxed by degrees as the week progressed, but it did not quite return to normal. Jason tried to encourage Kara in a few games which she had taken a great interest in but now she seemed to engage in them only to oblige him so that he might past the time quicker. She started to excuse herself by mid-afternoon to retire to the bedroom where she stayed until Logan came back. Jason was deeply saddened by this but he felt powerless to do anything about the situation.

On Friday morning the base was in a state of excitement. The general was back. He had not been on the base since they first invaded and he was expected to stay at Straveng for at least a week.

Logan was not surprised when he was summoned to report to his leader by mid-morning. However it was the first time that he felt worried about reporting to the general because suddenly he had something to hide.

As he entered the antechamber, Alfred was just leaving the general's office. While it was standard practice for him to give his report before Logan, they would normally share a few words in passing, but not today. Alfred could hardly meet his eyes and only nodded curtly at him before exiting the room.

Logan passed the time conversing with the general's assistant, Maydia Gaad while he waited to be called in. Maydia had started to work for the general at a very young age and Logan knew her better than most. She was often unseen but he had come to learn that wherever the general was, Maydia was not far away, quietly working her magic behind the scenes. In fact, it was a common belief that she knew more about the general than the man himself.

Despite being a few years older than him, Logan had always known that Maydia was taken with him. While he found it easy to talk with her he had never tried to move their relationship beyond a professional one. Thankfully, she had reciprocated.

Today his banter with her was done only half-heartedly as he was too preoccupied with the look on Alfred's face when he was leaving. Had the major gotten into trouble with the general over something? He taxed his brain to figure out if his own report was in order.

"The General will see you now," Maydia said, a little sad as always to lose his company.

General Atto Degan had once told him that he had been great friends with his parents and that he regarded Logan as a son. His awareness of this did not make it any easier to stand in the man's presence knowing that he had already begun a plot to betray him.

He spent about fifteen minutes debriefing Degan on his work and answering his astute questions. When the general seemed satisfied with his report, he came around to Logan's side of the desk and clapped him on the back. He walked with him slowly to the door, making Logan immediately uncomfortable. Despite his leader's profession of affection for him, this was the first time he was behaving so warmly towards him.

"Are you comfortably situated at Drumlin Hall?"

"Yes General. Thank you for asking."

"And what of the little possession you fought so hard to acquire? How is she?"

Logan felt his breath catch. In that simple inquiry, a light suddenly went on in his head. He remembered the face time conference he'd had with the general and Alfred a little over a month before. Degan had asked him if he had someone particular in mind to choose for his prize and he had said no. Yet it was clear from what his leader just said to him, and a previous conversation he'd had with Alfred at the officers' dinner, that they both knew he had lied.

"She is well in hand and knows her place sir," he said, recovering quickly. Logan hoped that by speaking in the same manner the general did about women, he could indicate that he had no more feelings for Kara than was expected.

Degan laughed out loud with appreciation. "That's my boy," he said, clapping Logan on the back again. "Alfred tells me that no one can claim to have laid eyes on her yet. Are you sure you have not killed her and dumped her body somewhere?"

Logan's heart was hammering. He knew beyond a doubt that this conversation he was having with the general was the reason Grute could not look him in the eyes after all. He had sold Logan out. Heat began to slowly rise up to his face. "N-No sir," he stuttered, caught off guard.

The general clasped him on the back again. "I'm joking," he said. "I'm sure it is just a case of you having such good taste that you are afraid she is going to be stolen away but have no fear of that. I will be there at the dinner tonight so you need not worry about a thing. I can't wait to meet her," he said at the door. Still smiling he opened it himself so that Logan could leave.

"Of course General," he murmured, and almost forgot to salute before he turned around and hurried away. Even though Maydia looked up from her desk when Logan reappeared, he was too caught up in his own thoughts to give her more than a cursory wave on his way out the door.

When Logan left, Degan walked slowly to the large window behind his desk. The Brock building stood thirty stories high and extended for another ten below ground. It overlooked not only the campus, but a good portion of the town of Brevika. The entire faculty was proud to have such an iconic building as a part of an already prestigious campus. He had donated all of the money himself under an alias to have it constructed and he was proud of how it had turned out. The Brock Building was now one of the most important buildings in his empire.

Degan could not help but take a deep breath and exhale with a self-satisfied smile. All that he surveyed from the very top floor of the building was only a miniscule fraction of what now belonged to him. Soon, it would all be his.

If only my father could see me now, he thought. He smiled a bit sadly as he took in the view. What he wished for was impossible because his father was dead. Atto had made sure of it by killing him with his own hands.

Maybe it was the conversations he'd had earlier with Grute and Dr. Quiste, and the thought of meeting Logan's property later that night that brought on the memories of his own mother and father. Whatever the reason, Degan allowed himself the opportunity to indulge in memories that had not surfaced in years.

It was about the time he first watched while his father fucked and brutally beat his mother. On that particular occasion, his father had not even bothered to close their bedroom door. Like a moth drawn to a flame, Atto had walked slowly in before he realized he was there.

He was old enough to have a full fledged hard on as he watched his father rape his mother. At one point, when his father looked over and saw him standing there, he just laughed and became even more barbaric towards his mother now that it was clear that he had an audience. Atto remembered feeling no remorse for his mother. He had already been taught by his father to despise her.

His father believed that a woman was made for only three things, fucking, serving a man and having his children. In his father's eyes, his mother had failed miserably at all three. Atto had always been a sore disappointment to him too and he had never hesitated to let him know it.

After that first time, he had continued to let Atto watch, but he never once offered him the opportunity to fuck his mother, even though it was clear that he wanted to. Later, when his father had continued to molest, and torture the female victims at the prison camp, Atto was still only allowed to watch - never to touch. Eventually he understood that this was just another way for his father to hurt him.

Even though Atto always felt that his mother was deserving of the abuse she received, he hated seeing the bruises that would quickly appear on her face and body. As a young man, he especially enjoyed indulging his senses in the physical beauty of a woman. When it was finally his turn to carry on his father's legacy, it became almost an obsession to discover ways to torture a woman without damaging her appearance. Since he shared this hobby with Dr. Quiste, he could always count on the man to come up with some new devilry for him to try out.

Today he reported that the latest device he was working on was finally ready for his use. Degan was therefore looking forward to his evening with uncharacteristic relish.

Chapter 30

Logan left the general's office, his heart pounding and the blood rushing to his head. He moved so automatically that he did not realize that he was heading to Drumlin Hall until he was entering the lobby. He felt only horror at his exchange with Degan. Not wanting to alarm Kara, he made an effort to compose himself before entering the apartment.

Jason and Kara were playing a game of Yunkle again. On his arrival, Kara jumped up, surprised to see him. She came to him immediately, but stopped short when she saw the look on his face.

"What is it Logan?" He had not done as good a job as he had hoped of concealing his worry. She saw right through him.

Taking her into his arms, he drew her desperately to him. "Your presence has been requested at the dinner tonight by the general himself."

Jason stood up anxiously. A shocked silence rang deafeningly through the apartment for what seemed like an eternity.

"I will have to take you Kara," Logan finally said gravely. Kara felt stunned, but eventually she nodded her head. "I will come back as soon as I can this afternoon so that I can properly prepare you. We have a lot to do. Work with Jason for now. He will tell you what is expected and how you will need to act tonight."

"I have shielded you from much because I did not think you had to endure it. You are likely to see and be exposed to atrocious things tonight. You must handle whatever happens to you with aplomb, otherwise I could lose you."

Kara could sense that he was very tightly

wound. Logan had not said that he too would be in danger but she knew that what happened that night could be detrimental to them both.

"Listen and do whatever Jason tells you no matter how debasing it may seem. Can you do that?" She nodded, and he kissed her again, right there in front of Jason. It was a desperate kiss, as if he meant to swallow her up and by such means hide her away from the rest of the world. "Please Kara, follow his instructions closely," he said, when he finally broke off the kiss. "Our lives could well depend on it."

Kara was truly alarmed. Logan looked so serious that all she could do was nod. He wanted to speak to Jason in private so she retired to the bedroom as if in a daze.

Jason knocked on the door of the bedroom within five minutes. Logan had already left the apartment, while he stood there his face clouded over with worry. It was Jason's expression that finally made her acknowledge the gravity of the situation.

The afternoon was spent with him drilling her repeatedly about one thing or another. What he asked of her filled her with trepidation but she put up no resistance, doing exactly as he directed. Kara was beginning to learn just how much he and Logan had sheltered her from.

Logan left the apartment his brain in overdrive as he headed back to the Brock building. For the duration of his time there, he focused only on what he needed to do for Kara. He had been putting a number of things in place to help her for the past week ever since he had decided that he needed to do a better job of protecting her. Now however, he felt it was better to be safe than sorry. That gave him only a few hours to complete an assignment that he was originally planning to handle over the next week.

As time wore on, he became even more agitated. Leaving work well before his normally appointed time, he made a short detour before going to the apartment.

Kara was clearly relieved to see him. She rushed to him, eager to be in his arms. "Oh Logan, how can you and Jason be cut from the same cloth as the rest of these people?"

"I honestly don't know. I have been wondering about that a lot myself lately," Logan admitted earnestly, crushing her to him as if he never intended to let her go. He closed his eyes and inhaled deeply of her scent.

Jason looked on quietly in the background. He had a direct view of Logan's face as he closed his eyes and gave himself over to Kara's embrace. The apprehension he saw there was enough to make him relieved for once that he was not in Logan's shoes.

He had enjoyed spending time with Kara. He had even relished the torture he felt at being in her presence without being able to have her. He hoped that nothing would change after tonight. But Kara was no ordinary woman. Jason was sure that they would all be holding their breath, hoping that they came out of this ordeal unscathed.

Logan questioned him closely about what he had covered with Kara and if he felt that she was prepared. "She has done well and will be fine if she manages to keep her wits about her," Jason said, trying to sound reassuring.

When Logan was fully satisfied with his debrief, he gripped Jason's hand and arm in a firm handshake. "Thank you for everything that you have done for me," he said with sincerity.

On impulse, Kara rushed forward too and hugged him. "Thank you," she said quietly into his chest.

Jason was stunned, but he slowly put his arms around her and held her gently. "You are most welcome." When she let go of him and went to stand at Logan's side, he continued. "I hope that tomorrow we can all have a good laugh about overreacting." Logan and Kara both smiled and nodded as he let himself out of the apartment.

They stood, arms around each other, looking at the closed door for long moments. Outside, Jason allowed himself a moment to lean against the wall of the corridor and close his eyes against his own anxiety and fear for Kara. There was nothing else he could do for her now other than what he had always done anyway - trust in Logan. He sent out his best wishes to them both before he continued down the hall to catch the elevator.

Chapter 31

"Come," Logan said suddenly, "we will have an early supper and then we must choose some clothes for you to wear this evening."

"I can't think about eating right now Logan," Kara cried incredulously. "I'm terrified."

Logan turned and faced her. He cupped her face with his hands. "I know that you are. I am too. But you must allow yourself to be led at every turn this evening. Okay?" She looked at him, her eyes brimming with tears that she fought to hold back. She raised trembling hands to his and shifted her face so that she could plant a sweet kiss in each of his palms.

There was a knock at the door, breaking them apart suddenly. It was the attendant with their supper cart. They sat down and ate slowly, Logan drilling her constantly about the roll she would be playing once they left the apartment. In truth, Jason had done a fantastic job of preparing her and Logan was beginning to gain confidence that Kara would be able to handle whatever situation was thrown at her.

He consoled himself with the fact that unless the general showed up with additional officers that outranked him, there would likely be no one at the dinner who could lay claim to her. Alfred was the only one who outstripped him in rank and Logan felt sure that Kara was not his type.

The fact that he might be overreacting about the event was always at the back of his mind. The general had given his assurance after all that Kara would not be taken from him. Still, he wanted to err on the side of caution. "Let's go pick out an outfit for you," he said, after he was satisfied that Kara had at least tried to force some of the food down.

Logan had ensured that Kara had an abundance of everything she would need, including clothes for various occasions. Despite the fact that he and others had done the shopping for her, she did not seem to mind. So far, she looked amazing in just about anything she wore. Logan was especially happy with his choice of negligees. They were absolutely ravishing on her and he was appreciative that she took her opportunities to wear them.

Today however, he was less than pleased that he could find nothing that muted her appeal enough to suit his liking. Already they had tried on at least five different outfits. "It's impossible for you to look bad in anything," he cried in exasperation, as she put on a floor length dress with a jacket.

She could not help it; she grinned, and came over to him where he was lounging on the bed, watching her dress and undress. "That is likely the best compliment I have ever received," she said, reaching down to kiss him.

It was too much for Logan who lay there watching her, his cock growing harder with each piece of skin that was first covered, and then revealed. He sat up on the edge of the bed while Kara stood between his legs. Placing his hands on her thighs, he hiked up the full length dress, gathering the fine material around her waist. He began kissing her flat abdomen, enjoying the feel of her silky skin on his lips. Kara inhaled sharply as she felt the familiar rush at his touch. She closed her eyes and placed both her hands in his thick, soft hair. She moaned throatily, immediately becoming wet with need for him.

Still holding up her dress around her waist, he worked with a free hand to slide her panties off. She quickly obliged him by removing them herself.

Pushing him gently to lay back on the bed, she worked quickly to remove his pants before she mounted him. Logan grunted softly as she slid completely down his shaft, taking all of him into her at once - just the way he liked to enter her. She reached down and kissed him tenderly. Despite his need to have her worry his shaft with her tight little cunt he was not willing to rush the moment. He kissed her back, long and passionately, trying to etch every detail of the moment into his memory.

Kara finally broke the kiss to trail her hot breath down to his chest before she rose off him. She began her erotic dance on his pole but this time it was not enough for Logan. He needed even more body contact with her. He rolled her onto the bed so that he was on top with her legs clamped around him.

Even though they were both more than ready to seek their release, Logan purposely slowed down their love making, choosing instead to kiss Kara's body all over; to touch and knead her soft, full breasts, and to savor her nipple one at a time in his mouth. He truly wished that he could stay right there for the rest of his life but his need was becoming urgent as the walls of her vagina pressed in around him.

He knew that she wanted him too so he began to move slowly, in and out of her. He watched her, never breaking eye contact. He wanted her to come first this time but since she too seemed to be holding off her pleasure for as long as she could, he wondered if he could manage to hold the strain. Just when he gave up all hope, he saw the wave of emotion glaze her eyes. The expression on her face was so sublime in her ecstasy that he gave up the fight instantly and exploded into her.

Logan felt as though he had poured his entire being into Kara. He gently rested his body on hers, still embedded inside her. She hugged him tightly. "I love you," he murmured, and Kara knew it to be true beyond a shadow of a doubt.

"I love you too," she whispered in his ear. They showered together and made love one more time before becoming serious about getting ready to go downstairs.

They decided on a pants suit for her while Logan insisted that she wore boots that were comfortable.

Figuring out how to arrange her hair gave Logan the most torture. When she wore it loose, she looked sexy and ravishing, while piling up her hair made her appear classy and sophisticated. They finally decided on pulling her hair back into a severe bun. She wore no makeup or adornments in the form of jewelry but none of that mattered anyway. Kara was most certainly a natural beauty.

When he was satisfied with her appearance, he kissed her nose. Logan himself looked smart as always in his full uniform. Holding her hands he brought them up to his lips and kissed them.

They stood for a long while silently regarding each other in the quite sanctuary of the apartment. Logan felt as if there was so much he wanted to say to her, but could not; or maybe he was just too afraid to walk out the door with her. Either way, they could not stay hidden away in there forever.

As if in silent agreement they took one more deep breath together and walked to the door.

Chapter 32

It felt strange to Kara to be outside the apartment. The last time she had stood in the corridor was when Jason first brought her to Drumlin Hall about two weeks ago. Despite feeling safe in the apartment for the most part, there were times when she had felt like it was her prison as well. Ironically, now that she was on the outside, all she wanted to do was to go back into it, but Logan had already positioned himself slightly behind her. He motioned her forward along the brightly lit corridor towards the elevator.

They met no one along the way yet Kara could feel the dread pooling in the pit of her stomach as Logan pressed the button for the elevator. She was not sure why she felt so anxious. Maybe it was because Logan and Jason had made such a fuss about what she was about to experience.

The elevator arrived much too quickly. They stepped in and she felt that she had just managed to take a single breath before it stopped ten levels down, on the ground floor of the building. "Here we go," Logan muttered, when the doors opened.

Although he and Jason had tried to caution Kara about what she could expect, they still could not have prepared her sufficiently for what immediately assailed her eyes. The lobby was packed with men and women and there was enough chatter to indicate a festive mood. The noise was coming mostly from the men while most of the women either looked scared, or whipped.

Kara directed her gaze to the floor as she had been instructed to do. Even so, she was still very aware of what was going on around her as she moved with wooden steps through the lobby of the building.

One officer had a fully clothed woman pinned against a stone pillar. He had hiked up her skirts and was fucking her savagely while no one seemed to pay the couple the slightest attention. Kara was horrified.

Another woman darted past her in fright as two men came running after her, laughing. Kara was immediately thrown back to the first day of the invasion when she had witnessed multiple women being molested on the sports field. She began to tremble and felt Logan's hand at her waist trying to steady her.

As they neared the entrance to the restaurant, Kara saw a woman just beyond the doors working hard at blowing a man who sat unconcernedly, drinking at the bar. He was fully clothed, except for his penis sticking out, semi-erect from his trousers. Another man, also sitting at the bar, was fondling a woman's breasts through her unbuttoned blouse while she stood with a dazed expression on her face. Kara could not help but think that the girl looked drugged.

"Captain Ursin. It is good to see you," someone said brightly, bringing Kara sharply back to her own reality. It was the maitre d'. He glanced appreciatively at Kara. "The general is in the private room at the back of the main dining room. He has asked for you to join him as soon as you arrive."

"Thank you Carl," Logan said easily, as he walked with her casually pass the man. Kara froze on the threshold of the establishment, unable to move, but Logan's firm hand was exactly what she needed to force herself forward.

There were people everywhere as Logan propelled her along. A number of the men called out or greeted him as he made his way to the back of the room. Some of them openly teased him about finally coming to the dinner with his prize while others simply congratulated him. It was almost too much for Kara to handle. She was grateful that her head continued to stay bent with her eyes to the ground in a fully submissive gesture.

As Logan moved with her towards the back of the dining room, he had begun to feel less apprehensive. He had never been in the room which the maitre d' had directed him to but he thought with relief that at least their meeting with the general would be a private one.

When he opened the door to the room he was completely unprepared for the many faces that looked up at him from a long table. Without missing a beat, he ushered Kara into the room and closed the door behind them.

Kara got a quick glimpse of a number of men sitting with women at their sides at a table. They had all stopped their conversation to look at them as they entered. She quickly moved her eyes to the floor again.

"Ah Logan," came a voice that was etched in here memory forever. "So glad you decided to join us. We were just about to start dinner. Some of the men were already making bets on whether you would join us or not. But since I am your general, I felt sure that the only bet I could make was that you would come. I am glad to see that you did not disappoint me."

Kara heard the approach of footsteps and saw shinny, black boots stop just before her. "And why would I not come when my general has personally invited me to be here?" asked Logan. Kara was surprised at how cool and calm he sounded.

"Exactly," said Degan. "Tell that to these disbelievers behind me. Alfred especially had no faith in you."

"Should I have had faith?" Alfred piped up defensively. "We all thought that he was fucking a ghost. No one could lay claim to setting eyes on his prize."

"And what a prize it is," said the general with exaggerated appreciation as he openly perused Kara's figure. He took her hand and pulled her forward and away from Logan. She felt a jolt of electricity at his touch but whereas the feeling was pleasant when Logan managed such a response from her, now she felt only a severe case of revulsion.

The general walked around her slowly while Kara could feel his eyes scrutinizing her body closely. It was worse than anything she had felt before when others ogled her. Evil seemed to emanate from every pore of this man. She could sense that Logan stood rigid by her side and despite her own panic, she felt sorry for him.

When he had made his way slowly all around her, General Degan placed his forefinger under her chin and raised her head so that he could look closely at her face. Kara did not raise her eyes. She wanted to cry out; to run away, but there was nowhere for her to go. "Look at me," he commanded, and she obeyed instantly.

It was a shock for her to look up and meet grey eyes which reminded Kara of death. They were boring into hers lasciviously as she tried her best to keep any expression out of her face. She was supposed to appear whipped and obedient but she was afraid, and it probably showed completely in her eyes.

"She is exquisite," said the general in awe. "No wonder you have not wanted to bring her forward."

Holding her chin, he turned Kara's head first this way, observing her closely. Then he turned her head the other way and repeated his observations as if she was merchandize that he was planning on purchasing. She felt completely soiled at his touch and scrutiny.

"Her skin is flawless. Just the way it should be," he murmured, deeply absorbed in his examination of her. He dropped his hand and faced Logan again. "I cannot abide marring the skin of someone you want to fuck. Come, you must sit with me," he said, and turning around, he walked back to the table where the servers were already bringing in the meal.

There were two empty seats on the right side of the general where he sat at the head of the table. As Logan was about to take the chair nearest to him, Degan laughed out loud. "As much as I enjoy your company Logan, tonight I am more in the mood for hers," he said, looking pointedly at Kara.

She was quickly placed next to him before they all sat down. Kara sat quietly and demurely never once lifting her eyes to meet anyone else's.

"She does seem completely whipped Logan. How did you manage it without physically hurting her?" Degan asked conversationally. Once again, despite all the preparation she'd had, she almost felt like gagging when she heard herself being referred to in this way.

"With all due respect sir, there is more than one way to bind a woman to you. Surely you of all people know that." There was a hint of amusement in his voice as he spoke. He paused hoping he would not have to elaborate but when the general continued to look at him expectantly he smiled smugly. "I have just managed to fuck her into submission," he said easily. The whole room erupted into the heavy laughter of male voices indicating that they were all listening closely to the conversation he was having with their leader.

Kara could not help but go red. Her breathing became difficult but she felt Logan's warm hand on her thigh, reassuring her beneath the table and she tried to relax a little.

"Well put," said the general. "And I can see from the way you tried to dress her tonight, you did not want to tempt anyone else into demanding that same privilege. But I am not sure that you have quite succeeded. You could have probably just thrown a bag on her and she would still exude that 'come fuck me 'til you drop' look." There was laughter again at the table but thankfully the attention was soon drawn away from her as the officers broached other topics with Degan.

Kara was amazed at the confidential nature of the issues that were being discussed while the Mindalean women were in attendance until she remembered that they were considered little better than dogs anyway. Since it was a sure thing that none of them would ever be allowed to live outside of the current environment there was no danger in the men discussing anything.

The general looked at her often, causing Kara to feel completely suffocated. "Does she eat like a bird because she is always so full of cock Logan?"

The comment had come out of nowhere and was designed to throw them both off their game. The room had gone suddenly quiet but Logan did not bat an eye as he continued to squeeze Kara's thigh.

"I believe so," he said without missing a beat. "She is more than happy to be my hen once it's my cock that's filling her up." Degan smiled appreciatively at Logan's quip and the other officers laughed as well.

Chapter 33

When the meal was finally over it was time for the diners to rejoin their comrades in the main room outside. "Wait a while Logan," the general said as he too got up to leave with Kara. "Alfred, can you make sure that we are not disturbed for a few minutes." Alfred nodded, ensuring that he was the last person to leave the room.

Degan got up from his chair and taking Kara by the hand, he motioned for her to stand up. Logan started to rise as well but the general indicated for him to stay seated. He maneuvered Kara until she stood a short distance from the table, but still facing Logan.

He had thought their ordeal almost over, but Logan begun to tense up again the moment General Degan took Kara's hand.

"I had intended only to have a good look at your prize, Logan," he said, "but even as I stand before her my cock is stiffening."

Logan ground his teeth together but said nothing. There was nothing he could say. In all the scenarios that had run through his mind it had never even occurred to him that he would have anything to fear from the general himself.

Kara looked as if the man had struck her a physical blow; she was as white as a sheet. "I would see more of her," Degan said. "Take the pins out of your hair," he commanded. Her eyes shot up and she looked at him in disbelief. It appeared as if she was having trouble comprehending him.

"Did you hear me?" he asked quietly, his voice full of menace. She stayed frozen.

Logan's heart was in his mouth. "Do as the

general commands you," he said as calmly and as unconcernedly as he could. Kara's hands flew immediately to her hair as she pulled the pins from it.

Degan chuckled. "Impressive; she obeys you like you are her general." For once Logan did not have a response for the man.

Kara's beautiful dark hair cascaded down, around her shoulders and the general inhaled sharply. He reached up slowly and buried his hand in her hair. Grabbing a handful he slowly pulled her head back.

The unexpected move made her mouth open slightly with surprise. The general immediately ducked his head and captured her mouth in a quick, thorough kiss. Kara could not help the whimper that escaped her. Her knees felt as if it would not support her but as quickly as it had begun, the kiss was over.

Logan's fingers were digging into his thighs below the table as he watched in agony. He entertained the thought of picking up one of the steak knives and plunging it into the general. Or coming up behind him and just snapping his neck. But he knew well enough that he was under close observation. He had already noted the recording lenses that were set up discreetly in the room. They were all on. If he attempted anything, he and Kara would both be dead before they could manage to get out of the room.

Before Degan moved away from her he dragged his tongue over her lips and looked lasciviously at her. She was now too petrified to even utter a sound; she saw her doom only too clearly in the man's blazing eyes.

"Take off your clothes," he commanded as he stepped away from her. Kara was shaking from fright but she hastened to obey. Had it not been for Logan sitting across from her looking as if he was in as much pain as she was in, Kara was sure she would have just tried to make a run for it. She felt that it would be better to be cut down by a laser blast than to be subjected to this humiliation. She stripped to her underwear and stopped.

She was still wearing her boots not realizing that she posed an even more tantalizing picture with just a bra, panties and her boots on. The general had stood back and watched her remove her clothing, but she had not dared to look once at Logan. She appeared completely vulnerable as the man took his time enjoying the sight of her.

Degan licked his lips making Logan close his eyes against the pain he felt. A number of options for their escape were running through his mind, but none of them would allow him to get Kara out of there safely. He had to believe that sooner rather than later, they would finally catch a break. All he could do for now was sit tight and try to endure.

"Take it all off," the general announced suddenly. Even though the command seemed to take a moment to register for Kara she bent down to remove her boots.

"No. Not those."

Kara froze. She slowly straightened up and removed her bra to expose her perfectly shaped breasts. Finally she took off her panties and stood before them both, completely nude except for the boots that ran halfway up her slender calves.

Logan closed his eyes again, his pain even more intense. He struggled to ensure that a groan did not escape him. Despite the fact that she was completely oblivious of the ravaging picture she presented, she could not have done a better job of providing a show if she had purposely set out to tantalize the man. He had always known that he could never hold on to Kara once she was out of the apartment and here was absolute proof of that.

She stood proudly before his leader's scrutiny, her arms at her sides instead of trying to cover any part of her as she continued to stare at the ground. One part of Logan was silently imploring her to look at him. He wanted to reassure her in some way but another part of him was afraid that one or both of them might do something that they would regret.

The general walked up to her and without warning, he placed the palm of his hand on her mound and sunk his middle and forefingers deeply into her. The move was so completely unexpected that Kara could not help but gasp. She felt his fingers move inside her, and he inhaled audibly before he pulled his fingers out, wet and slick. He raised it up to his nose and inhaled deeply. His eyes closed slowly appreciation quite evident on his face. Kara's body began to tremble even more with the strain of being so callously violated. She bit down on her lower lip as a sob threaten to escape her.

Logan's hands were clenched so tightly into fists in his lap that he could feel the tips of his fingers trying to bore holes right through his palms. When the general finally turned back to the table, he saw that Logan sat looking as pale as a wraith.

"Has this been so difficult for you Logan?" He asked in a surprised tone. "I hope you have not fallen in love with this bitch," he said scornfully.

It took a moment for Logan to compose himself enough to reply. "Of course not," he ground out eventually. "I had just thought to keep her to myself."

"Well it seems as though you have done a pretty good job of that so far. She is as tight as if she has never known another cock but yours."

The color flooded quickly to Logan's face and Degan did not miss it. He whipped around and looked closely at Kara who now stood with her head bent, quietly sobbing.

"She was a virgin?" he asked in surprise. He turned back to Logan who had no choice but to nod reluctantly.

"Now that is truly amazing," said the general, looking impressed. "I want her Logan," he said simply, but with conviction.

Logan flew up from the chair upsetting it so that it crashed to the ground with a loud noise. "No!" he cried. Degan looked surprised at his response. Logan found himself fighting for control and some way to salvage the situation before it was too late. It was hard to reason through the haze of rage and fear that clouded his mind. He made another concerted effort to bring himself under control. "I only meant that it would be difficult for me to give her up," he said more submissively.

His leader's expression softened noticeably. "I understand," he said seriously.

"It must be amazing to fuck her tight cunt every night. Maybe we can come to some sort of an arrangement where you will not have to give her up entirely. I have never thought to share a woman before but you are like blood to me. We might be able to ramp up our pleasure significantly if we take her together."

Kara's legs suddenly gave way and she sank to the ground. The horror of what this despicable man had just said so insouciantly was too much for her. Not only was he going to rape her, but he was going to force Logan to do it as well - at the same time! In that moment Kara felt very alone and completely petrified.

The little food that she had managed to eat before they had come down to the restaurant rose to the back of her throat. She was relieved for the preoccupation of trying to swallow so that she did not throw up at the man's feet. She knew that Logan could do nothing about what was happening and she did not dare to look at him least he lose his mind and did something stupid.

It was one thing if she must be put through this ordeal but she was not going to be responsible for him losing his life foolishly while trying to protect her in this no win situation. For the first time in his life Logan stayed frozen and unable to think. He felt sick to the pit of his stomach. Time seemed to slow to a crawl as the general turned and glanced down at Kara on the floor. Her reaction to his news did not appear to faze him in the least.

"Bring her to my suite tonight and we will enjoy her pleasures together. Dr. Quiste has been working on something extra special for just such an occasion."

Logan felt as if he was slowly coming up for air. Had he heard the general correctly? Was this the break he was looking for? He could not believe that the man was willing to put off his diabolical plans until later, but he was most definitely relieved. He could see clearly that the general was fully aroused and he knew something about the self-control that was needed to delay the pleasure of taking Kara.

If the general had tried to rape her, Logan would have had no choice but to kill him which would have meant forfeiting the lives of both him and Kara. Still, such a fate would have been better than the alternative of watching him molest her. The general had also made mention of something Dr Quiste was working on to use on Kara. Logan did not even want to speculate on what that could be.

General Atto Degan adjusted his crotch with some difficultly and grabbed his hat from the table, indicating that the interview was over. Logan allowed his eyes to fall on Kara where she lay trembling with shock. "I will expect you at midnight."

"Yes General," was all Logan could manage as the man left the room, closing the door behind him without a backward glance.

Chapter 34

Logan forced himself to walk unhurriedly around the table to where Kara was huddled on the ground in an almost fetal position. As he made as if to help her up off the floor, he took the opportunity to whisper discreetly in her ear. "It is going to be okay Kara. You just have to hold it together a little longer."

She nodded at him but she wondered if he was going mad. Did he not just hear what that horrible man had said? The thought of being taken not only by Logan but the creepy general too – at the same time, did not qualify as everything being okay to her. She glared at him as she climbed to her feet.

Logan stepped away from her not daring to reach out once to help her with her clothes while the recording lenses were still on but he continued to implore her with his eyes to keep her head. Kara remembering again what he had said about Straveng having eyes and ears everywhere, composed herself with a tremendous effort and focused on getting her clothes on. Logan could see that her hands were trembling as she worked but he was proud that she was doing a good job of keeping her wits about her.

When she was done he took her by the elbow and guided her out of the room and through the restaurant. He moved quickly, pushing her along in front of him. "I need to get some fresh air," he said nonchalantly and loudly enough for the benefit of anyone who was listening. Instead of leading them back to the elevator though, he moved with her to the revolving door that led outside.

"We are probably being watched," he said, in a low voice as they left the building. "Just continue behaving as calmly as possible." He put a possessive arm around her waist and walked into the night at what he hoped was a leisurely pace.

Kara was livid though. How did Logan expect her to be calm about what she had just been through? "What are we going to do?" she asked her voice shaky with fright.

"I need to get you away as soon as possible," Logan whispered. But what exactly did that mean? Kara thought in exasperation. Seeing that she was about to face her doom in just a couple of hours she was quite irritated by how calm Logan appeared, and how vague his response was.

She was about to direct a tirade at him when she recalled Jason's words earlier that day. *Trust in Logan if all else fails.* At the time he had said it to her, Kara thought he was only trying to give her false hope. Yet here was her chance to do exactly what Jason had advised her to do, and so far he had not led her wrong about anything. If Jason trusted Logan so explicitly, there was no reason why she shouldn't too.

Alfred had stood by the door of the private room until the general emerged and spoke to him in a low voice. "You were right to bring this matter to my attention. He is far too taken with this bitch." Degan paused but then blurted out through clenched teeth: "I could not be any more disappointed in him."

Alfred was inordinately pleased to hear that his hunch about Logan and his prize had paid off. He had gone to see the general that morning to give his report as usual but at the end of it he had hesitated, struggling with whether or not he should raise the issue concerning Logan. He had finally capitulated and alerted his leader to his suspicions. Alfred was pleased to see that Degan had taken them seriously.

"He is young and apt to make mistakes," Alfred said, trying to seem neutral and somewhat indulgent of Logan. He knew that the captain was one of the general's few favorites, and he did not want to appear as if he had a bone to pick with him. Inside however he felt like jumping for joy. He despised Logan and was only too happy to stand and watch on the sidelines as he was pulled from his pedestal.

"Of course, youth is reckless," Degan agreed. "He probably still thinks that he can be with whomever he pleases. But I see what you mean about her being dangerous, she can certainly mess with a man's convictions. I have just had my own little taste of that. She will have to go, of that I am convinced. But there is no reason why I should not have a little fun with her first. I want to make sure that Logan is taught a lesson he will never forget. By the time I am through with that little slut he will want to have nothing more to do with her.

The End